About the Author

Jean Ure had her first book published while she was still at school and immediately went rushing out into the world declaring she was AN AUTHOR! But it was another few years before she had her second book published and during that time she had to work at lots of different jobs to earn money. As well as writing, Jean really loves drama, acting and the theatre and in the end she went to drama school to train as an actor. Some of her ideas for the *Stevie Silver* stories come from her experiences there. Jean has written more than eighty books, and you can read about some of them on her website, which you can find at **www.jeanure.com**

Jean now lives in Croydon with her husband and their family of seven rescued dogs and four rescued cats.

Also by Jean Ure from Orchard Books

Stevie Silver – Star Light

Girls Stick Together
Girls are Groovy
Boys are OK!
Pink Knickers aren't Cool

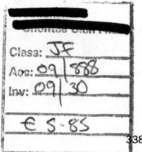
ORCHARD BOOKS
338 Euston Road, London NW1 3BH
Orchard Books Australia
Hachette Children's Books
Level 17/207 Kent Street, Sydney, NSW 2000, Australia
ISBN 1 84121 780 8
First published in Great Britain in 2006
A paperback original
Text © Jean Ure 1999 and 2006
The stories in this book were first published
as part of the *Sandy Simmons* series
The right of Jean Ure to be identified as the author of
this work has been asserted by her in accordance with
the Copyright, Design and Patents Act, 1988
A CIP catalogue record for this book is available
from the British Library
1 3 5 7 9 10 8 6 4 2
Printed in Great Britain

Stevie Silver

STAGE STRUCK

JEAN URE

ORCHARD BOOKS

Contents

Stevie Silver – Superstar

Chapter 1

Hi! My name's Stevie Silver and I'm a student at the Starlight Stage School.

People are always asking me what it's like, being at a stage school. The answer is, it's brilliant! Totally and utterly *brilliant*.

Another thing they ask is, "Do you get to do acting all the time?" The answer to that is...I wish! During the day we have to do ordinary lessons (groan) just like anyone else. It's usually not until the end of the day, plus sometimes on Saturday mornings, that we get to do all the exciting stuff. All the important stuff! Singing and dancing. Voice, make-up, mime.

Mime is acting without words, like sign language. Sometimes I talk in sign language at home, just to annoy my brother. His name is Thomas, and he won't answer if you call him Tom. But that's OK; I respect how he feels. My real name is Evie, which I absolutely

HATE. Evie Lynn Silver. Ugh! Yuck! I ask you! When I decided to be an actor I changed it to *Stevie*. My stage name! Everyone calls me Stevie, even Mum and Dad. *I won't ever let anyone call me anything else.*

Names are so important! My best friend at Starlight is called Stephanie, which she reckons is just totally naff, so her stage name is Steffi, or Steff. Sometimes we are Stevie and Steff. Sometimes we are Steffi and Steve. We think that's pretty neat!

Steff is blonde and bubbly with sparkly bright blue eyes. She is not terribly slim, but she is what I would call *cuddly*. I, on the other hand, am not terribly *tall*, and my hair is brown and not very long – unlike Steff's, which is so long she could practically sit on it. I am quite prettyish, I think, though nowhere near as pretty as Steff. But I don't mind! I once heard someone say that I had "oodles of personality". You need personality if you are going to be a star. Which I am!

Steffi's mum and dad are both in show business. I really envy her that. My mum and dad are nice but quite ordinary, though my Auntie Lily was a student at Starlight when she was my age, which is one of the reasons I wanted to go there. She'd told me so much about it! All the fun she'd had, and all the shows she was in.

Steffi and me have two other friends that we hang out with. They are called Rosa and Dell. Rosa is tiny.

She whizzes about like a spider, very quick and light. She is not pretty, but she has this BIG voice and can sing in tune, either way down low, or way up high.

She is going to sing in musicals one day.

Dell is the prettiest of any of us. Her dad is French and her mum is West Indian, so we all think she is very exotic. Like a golden pineapple, or one of those fruits that when you cut them open they look like stars. She has these huge liquid eyes and creamy skin and gorgeous glossy hair. Dell is really beautiful. She doesn't yet know whether she wants to be an actor or a dancer, but Auntie Lily says that when you have looks like that you can do almost anything you want.

What is good about Dell is that she is not vain. We wouldn't be friends with her if she was vain.

There's a girl in our class who is. Vain, I mean. Her name is Starlotta. (Can you believe it? *Starlotta*?) She is always tossing her hair and rolling her eyes and making like she's *soooo* much better than anyone else. She is not one of our friends.

There are also boys, of course. Some of them aren't too bad. Some of them are even quite nice. Ricky Robson, for instance, and Buster Wells. Auntie Lily says that Buster is going to be a heart-throb when he grows up.

Ricky is a comedian; he makes people laugh. He has a head shaped like a turnip, and sometimes he twizzles his fingers in his hair and makes it go into

11

a point on top. It just kills me when he does that!

One day in my first term, Miss Todd, who is our drama teacher, announced that all of our year was to be auditioned for parts in a Christmas show. I was thrilled! I'd only been there two months and already I was going for an audition!

I went rushing home to tell Mum about it. She said, "How exciting! What is it for? What's the show?"

I told her that it was called *The Magic Toyshop* and that it was opening on Boxing Day.

Mum said, "Oh, dear! So you'd have to work Boxing Day?"

"You always do, if you're in a show," I said. "But we'd be sure to get comps, so you could all come and see it."

Comps are free tickets. I learnt that from Steff.

"Go and see a kids' show?" jeered Thomas.

Honestly! He's only a year older than me. But Thomas reckons he's dead superior.

"Of course we'd all go and see it!" said Mum. "You wouldn't want to miss your sister in her very first part, would you?"

"She hasn't got it yet," said Thomas.

I said, "Thank you very much. That's all I need."

"You mustn't be disappointed if they don't offer you anything," warned Mum. "After all, it's only your first term. And there'll be lots of other opportunities."

I said, "Oh, I'm not really expecting to get

anything." All airy and unconcerned. "I'm only going along 'cos Miss Todd said it would be good experience."

"That's the way to look at it," agreed Mum.

But however much I pretended not to care, I had this tight little knot of excitement inside me. I kept seeing my name up in lights.

* * * * * * * * * * * *
THE MAGIC TOY SHOP
* * * * starring * * * *
STEVIE SILVER
* * * * * * * * * * * *

It was only a daydream. I knew I wasn't really going to get a star part. We weren't even auditioning for star parts. Just the little bits and bobs, as Miss Todd called them.

"But everyone has to start somewhere," she said. "Remember, even the biggest stars have played bits and bobs in their time."

If I couldn't even get a bit or a bob, I might just as well lie down and *die*.

Steffi felt exactly the same. Even though she'd been at the school two years longer than me, she'd never gone for a real professional audition before. "Miss Todd always said we were too young."

So this was the first time for both of us! Steff came

back to tea after school one day and we told each other how we simply *had* to get into the show.

"Everyone gets into a show at Christmas," said Steff.

Mum seemed a bit alarmed. "I really don't think you should build up your hopes too much. There must be hundreds of people auditioning."

"No." Steffi pulled a face. "Just us and the Monas!"

Mum looked puzzled. "What moaners?"

"The Mona Wests," I said.

The Mona West Academy is our greatest rival. A silly tinpot little school in another part of London. We are always bumping into a gaggle of Monas when we go for auditions.

"I shall just d*ie*," said Steff, "if I don't get in!"

"Me, too!" I wailed.

"Life just wouldn't be worth living!" Steffi snatched at the Queen of Sheba, who is one of our cats. "Oh, Sheba, bring me luck!" she begged.

I immediately looked round for Bunter, who is our other cat, but he was nowhere to be seen. He was probably up in the airing cupboard, snoozing. In any case, you need a black cat for luck and Bunter is blue. Well, grey blue, so it probably wouldn't have worked.

Afterwards, when Steffi had gone home, Thomas said, "What cheek! Using our cat to wish herself luck."

I tried not to let myself think that it was an omen, but I couldn't help wondering whether it meant that Steff was going to get a part and not me...

Chapter 2

There was only a week to go before the auditions. Miss Todd said that we were all to work extra specially hard and be prepared for whatever they might ask us to do.

"Dance, sing a song...you must each have something ready. Just in case."

She said that what they were mainly looking for was dancers, so every afternoon, at the end of ordinary school, we practised some dance routines in the big dance studio, either with Miss Merchant or with Mrs Kazinsky.

Miss Merchant is really nice because she encourages you and doesn't yell, but when it's Mrs Kazinsky, **BEWARE!!!** She takes us for ballet, and she is frightening. We call her Madam. She runs at people with her stick, shouting, "Shake out those shoulders! Tighten that tummy!" and whacking as she goes.

Poor Steff is always being told to hold her tummy in. It's so unfair! She can't help being a bit plump. I don't like ballet very much. Tap is my favourite.

"I shouldn't worry," said Dell soothingly, after one of Madam's classes when she'd prodded and poked at me till I was sore all over. "They're not going to want you to dance the Dying Swan."

"I feel like a dying swan," I groaned.

"You don't look like one," said Starlotta. She cackled. "You look more like a squashed toad!"

She's always making these kinds of remarks. She thinks they're funny. "Squashed toad yourself," I muttered.

It was all I could think of at the time. Afterwards, when it was too late, I wished that I had called her a cross-eyed ostrich. She looks like an ostrich. She has this great long bendy neck and this big beaky mouth and huge enormous eyes with flippy-flappy eyelashes that bat at you.

You don't notice it quite so much when she's dressed; but when she's in her leotard she looks really peculiar. I don't know why she gives herself such airs!

"It's because her uncle's on TV and he's famous," said Rosa.

"So are Steffi's mum and dad," I said. "Steffi doesn't give herself airs."

Rosa said that was because Steffi's mum and dad

were just 'ordinary actors' that most people hadn't heard of. "Not many actors get to be famous."

I'm going to be! I'm going to be a S*T*A*R*.

"Aim high," Auntie Lily always says. And that is what I am doing!

Every day after school I rushed back home to have my tea, then raced upstairs to my bedroom to practise for the audition. I didn't even watch television! Mum called up to me, "Stevie, it's *Dweebs*." But I wouldn't even stop to watch *Dweebs*, even though it's my favourite. I just had to get a part in the Christmas show!

And then one evening Dad came upstairs and said, "Stevie, this is quite enough of all this. All this thumping and banging. You'll bring the ceiling down."

"But, Dad!" I wailed. "I've got to practise!"

"Not all night long. It's becoming ridiculous. I want you to stop. Right now!"

Mum agreed. She said, "You can practise for one hour after tea. You can do it in the sitting room."

Thomas immediately shouted, "What about my homework?"

"You can do your homework upstairs."

"But I always do it *down*stairs! I'm used to doing it downstairs!"

"Yes, and I need to practise for far longer than an hour," I said. "An hour isn't anywhere near long enough."

"Oh, for goodness' sake!" snapped Mum. "Just be quiet, the pair of you! You're far more indulged than most kids. Just think yourselves lucky!"

So then we both sulked.

Thomas said, "You're like an elephant, crashing about up there. If you hadn't made such a row, Dad wouldn't have stopped you. Then I'd still be able to do my homework where I always do my homework!"

I said, "Oh, bother your stupid homework!"

"Yes, and bother your stupid dancing!" roared Thomas.

I think it is true to say that none of my family really understands me.

When the day of the audition arrived I was dead nervous and didn't want to eat any breakfast, but Mum insisted. She said, "You can't be at your best on an empty stomach."

Dad wanted to know if this was the Big Day. I said that it was and he said, "Well, in that case I'll be thinking of you," and gave me a kiss and a hug.

At the very last minute Thomas came rushing up with Sheba. I was so surprised! I hadn't expected anything from Thomas.

"Here!" He pushed her at me. "Take her! Have a wish. Go on! Black cat, it's lucky."

So I cuddled her and asked her to bring me luck, but I wasn't sure it would work, because maybe Steff had already taken all the luck there was?

The auditions were held in a studio near Covent Garden. There was just us, and the Monas. I'd never met any Monas before, but Starlotta had and she said they were rubbish.

"Total rubbish!"

I tried to feel comforted, but they were all laughing and talking in really loud voices and seemed tremendously sure of themselves. They have this yucky yellow uniform, which SHOUTS at you. (Ours is a lovely deep crimson.)

We were all told to go and change into our dance clothes, and guess what? The Monas' leotards were yellow, too!

"Like dog sick," whispered Rosa, and that made me giggle and feel a bit better.

As soon as we'd changed we were called into the studio, and a tubby man with a beard and a woman dressed in a silver top and black leggings introduced themselves to us. The man was called Melvyn Twelvetrees and the woman was called Buzz Peabody. Melvyn Twelvetrees was the producer. I'd never met anyone as important as a producer before and I started to come over all nervous again, but apart from the beard he was quite nice.

First thing that happened, we were all given numbers to wear. Next thing was, we all had to get in line so they could look at us. Then after a bit Buzz Peabody started pointing at people and telling them to "Go over there" or "Join that group in the corner."

There were eight groups in all. Some were just boys, and some were just girls. The biggest group was Group C, which was boys and girls mixed. Group C was the one that I was in. I couldn't decide whether it was good to be in the biggest group or whether it meant that we were all going to be told, "No, thank you."

Rosa was in it with me and we flashed each other anxious glances. Ricky was also in it. But Ricky is funny and has a head like a turnip. Why was I in the same group as him?

Dell was in Group D. Group D was tiny, and it was all girls. So was Group E, which was where Steffi had been put. Rosa whispered at me, "We've got all the smallest people in our group." She was right! A Mona who was standing just nearby must have heard her. She screwed up her face and hissed, "It's mice."

I thought, mice? What was she talking about? But I didn't have time to puzzle over it. Buzz Peabody was asking Group C to come into the middle and for all the others to sit down and wait their turn. She told us that the lady at the piano was going to play some scurrying music.

"I'd like you all to scurry. Can you do that?"

The Mona rolled her eyes. "Told you!"

The piano started up and we all scurried like mad, round and round the studio. Part of the time I scurried like a mouse, in case the Mona was right and that was what they wanted; and part of the time I tried to scurry like Mrs Kazinsky would have made us, with pointed toes and good turn-out.

All the time we were scurrying, Buzz Peabody and Melvyn Twelvetrees were murmuring to each other and making marks on sheets of paper.

"Deciding our fate," mouthed the Mona, as we scurried past each other.

Almost before I knew it, the audition was over. The producer said, "Thank you very much, Group C! You can go and get changed, now. We'll be in touch."

And that was that! That was all they wanted. Just a little bit of scurrying.

"Mice," hissed the Mona.

She seemed really peeved about it. I couldn't imagine why. I said to Rosa, "I wouldn't mind being a mouse! Not if it means acting in a real West End show."

Rosa agreed with me. "We can't all get to play proper parts," she said.

I really wished she hadn't said that. It nagged at me all the way home. Wasn't a mouse a proper part?

Steffi was with me. (We always travel together on the tube.) She was all bright and bubbly, same as usual.

"How d'you think we did? I think we did quite well! I was watching you, and you scurried loads better than the rest of them. You and Rosa," she added, loyally. "It was a pity you didn't get to see me. I think I did OK, but it's difficult to know."

"You'll be all right," I said. "You'll get in."

"Oh! Do you think so?" She turned to me, eagerly. "Do you really honestly think so?"

"Yes, 'cos you asked Sheba to bring you good luck," I said.

"You could have asked her as well!" said Steff.

"You can't *keep* asking them," I said. "It only works for one person."

Just for a minute, Steff looked really crestfallen. Then she squeezed my arm and said, "We'll both get in. You'll see!"

Chapter 3

A whole week had passed since the audition and we still hadn't heard who had got in and who hadn't. Starlotta, who always claimed to know everything, said that not hearing was a good sign.

"No news is better than bad news."

But no news was starting to make us grow really tense. Rosa was biting her nails and Steff kept chewing her hair. If mine had been long enough to reach as far as my mouth, I would probably have chewed mine, as well. Instead I kept pressing a finger against the tip of my nose and turning it up like a pig's, which is this silly thing I tend to do when I'm nervous.

Dell said, "You'll get stuck like that and then you'll be sorry." And she made piggy noises at me: "Oink, oink!"

Dell was the only one of us who didn't seem terribly

bothered. When the rest of us said that we would die if we didn't get in, Dell just shrugged. Her mum was having a new baby and Dell was far more excited about that than she was about the audition. We told her she was mad.

"Anyone can have a baby," said Steff. "Not everyone can get into the Christmas show!"

The weekend was the worst part. I didn't have anyone I could talk to. Not anyone that would understand. Steff had gone to visit her nan, and Dell and Rosa live miles the other side of town. So there I was. Stranded. All on my own. Just Mum and Dad and Thomas. It wasn't the least bit of use moaning and wailing at *them* and saying I would die.

I tried it, Saturday morning at breakfast. I went, "Oh, I can't bear it! I've got to live through the whole weekend without knowing! And then if I get there on Monday and Miss Todd says I'm not in...I shall die! I shall just die!"

You'd think my family would have shown at least a little bit of sympathy. But Mum just pushed a bowl of gluggy porridge at me and said, "Get that down you. It'll do you good." And Dad laughed and told me not to be so over the top, and Thomas went, "*Oh!*" in a silly shrieky sort of voice. "I shall die! I shall just *die!*" And then he made his eyes go big like saucers and fell in a pretend faint on top of the table and knocked the milk jug over. Dad caught it just in time.

He said, "Watch it, sunshine! I thought it was your sister who's supposed to be the actress round here?"

"Actor," I snapped, "if you don't mind."

After that I didn't talk to them any more. I rang Rosa and we had a good long moan at each other and I felt a bit better.

And then, on Monday, we heard. The news was buzzing all about the classroom even before first break.

"The list is up! The list is up!"

As soon as the bell rang we all went rushing down to look at the notice board and see if our names were there. Rosa, who is good at burrowing, burrowed her way to the front and called out the news.

"Dell – yesssss! Steffi – yesssss! Me – yesssss! Stevie – yesssss!"

"But what parts?" screeched Steff.

Rosa elbowed a few people out of the way. (Rosa has great elbows. Very sharp and pointy.) We strained to hear her above all the cries.

"French Doll...Dell. Rag Doll...Steff. Clockwork Mice...me and Stevie. The Mona was right!"

"Hooray!" Steffi grabbed me and swung me round. "We're in, we're in, we're all of us in!"

We galloped together up the corridor, chanting as we went: "We're in, we're in, we're all of us in!"

One of the teachers came out of the staffroom and snapped, "What do you girls think you're doing?"

There are very strict rules at Starlight. We are not supposed to run or jump or make a noise in the corridor.

"Stop it this instant, or I'll put you on report!"

Ho! She needn't think we cared. We'd been to an audition and we'd got parts!

It wasn't until later that I managed to have a proper look at the list. There was:

1 French Doll
1 Rag Doll
3 Dancing Dolls
3 Action Men
2 Teddy Bears
4 Soldiers
1 Fairy
1 Acrobat
and *16 Clockwork Mice*.

Now I knew why the Mona had been so grumpy. Being a mouse was like being part of the *corps de ballet*. Just one out of sixteen. It wasn't a real part at all!

When I got home that afternoon Mum said, "Well? Don't keep me in suspense! Did you hear?"

I said, "Yes. I'm a mouse."

"Oh, that's wonderful!" cried Mum. "That calls for a celebration!"

Mum was really excited. She went round telling everyone. "Stevie's playing a mouse in *The Magic Toy Shop*!" She rang up both my nans and Auntie Lily. She rang up my dad at his office.

"Guess what? Your clever daughter's got her first part!"

That evening we went up the road to the Pizza Express and Mum and Dad had a bottle of wine and let me have a sip (only I didn't like it). They clinked their glasses and drank a toast to, "Our little mouse." Even Thomas rather gruffly said, "Congratulations."

I told Mum I was only one of sixteen, but it didn't stop her being excited. She still seemed to think it meant that I was going to be some kind of big star. Which I am going to be, of course. One day. But no way was I going to be a big star playing a clockwork mouse!

I tried ever so hard not to be jealous of Dell and Steffi, because they are my friends and being jealous is horrid. All the same, it was really difficult having to sit in rehearsals and watch as they did their solos. The only other main soloists were the Fairy (one of the Monas) and the Acrobat, who was Buster. I didn't mind about Buster because he is a boy and very athletic; and I didn't mind about the Fairy as I am not very fairylike. More of an imp, my dad says. But even Starlotta was a Dancing Doll. Starlotta! That cross-eyed ostrich!

What made it worse was that everyone except the Mice was taught their steps by Buzz Peabody. But as soon as the Mice came on, Buzz Peabody disappeared and someone called Ben took over. Ben was young and friendly and nice, but we all knew that he wasn't really important. So of course that made us feel that we weren't very important, either. Dell and Steffi did their best to cheer us up.

"It's because you're small," said Dell. "They always choose the smallest ones to be mice."

Steff agreed with her. She said I would still have been a mouse even if she hadn't used Sheba to wish herself luck. Needless to say, the other two immediately wanted to know what she was talking about. When I told them, Rosa said, "Well! That wasn't very fair, using Stevie's cat."

"I didn't think," admitted Steff. But then she added, "I'm afraid you have to be tough to survive in this business."

It was one of the things her mum and dad had told her. She was always quoting it at us.

"You have to look out for yourself, 'cos if you don't, nobody else will."

"So, like, you mean you steal people's cats?" said Rosa.

"I didn't steal it. I just saw her there. So I picked her up."

"I think it's a bit mean if people can't get good luck

from their own cats," said Rosa.

"Oh, look, I'm sorry!" said Steff. "But, honestly, it wouldn't have made any difference. It's not that me and Dell are any better than you. Just that we're taller." She turned to Dell. "Isn't that right?"

"Yeah. Absolutely." Dell nodded, and her hair bounced and shone.

Steffi came up to me later. She slipped her arm through mine and whispered, "You're not mad at me, are you? Because of Sheba?"

"No," I said. "I'm just mad at me for not thinking of it first"

Or for not being taller.

Or maybe both.

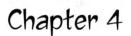

Chapter 4

I made up my mind that if I had to be a mouse, then I would be the *best* mouse. I would be the mouse that everybody noticed, so that people would go home afterwards and say, "Did you see that one little mouse? She really stood out!"

Even Buzz Peabody and the producer would notice me. They would make a note by my name: *Future Star!!!* And next time when they wanted someone to do a solo, they would ring up Starlight and ask for me specially.

"We'd like to have Stevie Silver, please! We still remember her wonderful mouse."

I went to the pet shop, where they had mice for sale. They were so sweet! Little furry, nibbling creatures with tiny pink hands and shell-shaped ears. I would have loved to have one, but Mum wouldn't let me. She said it was cruel to keep mice in a cage, and what about the cats? "They'd terrify the poor thing!"

I knew she was right, and that I would have to be content with just looking. I studied those mice for ages! I watched the way they moved, so quick you'd almost have thought they were on rollers. I watched the way their noses quivered and their whiskers twitched. And then I rushed away to practise.

I practised being mouse-like everywhere I went! I scuttled up the road to the tube station. I sat and nibbled on the tube. I twitched my whiskers in class. I rubbed my paws round my ears, the way I'd seen the mice do in the pet shop. I scurried and skittered in the playground, and flittered and pounced as I ran up the stairs.

People laughed at me, but I didn't care! Starlotta curled her lip. She said, "A mouse is a mouse. They don't want supermice!"

"How do you know?" said Dell. She's always sticking up for people.

"If they'd wanted supermice they'd have said so. They'd have said, clockwork mice and supermice."

I tried not to take any notice of Starlotta; she's quite a mean sort of person. Unfortunately, though, it did seem that she was right. They didn't want supermice. When I tried doing a bit of twitching and nibbling on stage, I got told off for it.

Ben stopped the rehearsal and said, "That mouse

there! Number Four. What are you doing, petal?" He called everyone petal. "Have you got an itch?"

So embarrassing! Starlotta wasn't there, but some of the Monas sniggered.

I said, "No, I'm being a mouse."

Ben said, "We're all being mice, petal!"

"Yes, I know," I said. "But I'm giving mine some character."

"Sorry, petal! Wrong time, wrong place. Just stick to the steps you've been taught. OK?"

Back in the changing room, Rosa tried to comfort me.

"You really have to be a soloist before they let you do your own thing. They like the rest of us to be all the same."

I just scowled at her and went stalking off. I suppose it was a bit unkind, really; I mean, she was only trying to help. But I didn't want to be the same as everyone else! I wanted to be me. I wanted to be a S*T*A*R*.

Later on, Ben came up to me. He said, "You're a bit of a comic, aren't you?" He didn't say it nastily. He said it as if he thought that being a bit of a comic might be quite a good thing to be.

I said, "Am I?"

Ben laughed and said, "Yes, you are! But there's a time and a place, petal. Don't worry, your time will come!"

I felt better after that. I rushed home and excitedly reported the news to Mum. "I'm a bit of a comic!"

"Well, I could have told you that," said Mum.

It's funny, but I'd never thought of it before.

At the end of the first fortnight of rehearsals, the understudy list went up. There were sixteen proper parts and sixteen mice, so all of us that were mice had to understudy someone. I got to understudy Steff!

This was good in one way, as it meant we could go round to each other's house and she could teach me the Rag Doll dance so that I could practise it. Then when we had our first understudy call, I would already know all the steps and everybody would be just *sooo* impressed!

But in another way it wasn't so good. I wasn't sure that I liked being my best friend's understudy. Dell giggled and said, "If ever you get to go on, they'll have to do up your costume with safety pins!"

She meant because of Steff being plump and me being skinny.

"Don't worry," drawled Starlotta. "It never happens. Understudies never get to go on."

"She'd have to if Steffi got sick."

"People don't get sick," said Starlotta. "Not in this business. You can't afford to."

I knew she was right. All the same, I couldn't help daydreaming...it wasn't that I wanted Steffi to get sick. It would be terrible to want your own best friend to get sick. But imagine if she did!

In the end I had to stop myself thinking about it.

The Rag Doll's dance was slow, and a bit floppy. Quite different from the dance of the French Doll, which was very fast and sizzling. Very zippy-zappy! I could see why they'd given the Rag Doll to Steff. She's quite soft-looking and sort of...well...bendy. You could believe, sometimes, that she has sawdust instead of bones.

I couldn't imagine why they'd chosen me to understudy her, as I am not in the least soft or bendy. Mum says I am quite a "tough little cookie". I decided that most probably they'd just picked on anybody at all and didn't really care. Understudies aren't that important. As Starlotta said, they never get to go on.

The dress rehearsal was on Christmas Eve. The weekend before, Steff came round to tea. She only lives five minutes away, so we see quite a lot of each other out of school. Before she arrived, Thomas said, "Is this the one you're understudying?"

I said, "It's Steffi." He knew perfectly well who she was.

"Would you like me to make a wax dummy and stick pins in it for you?"

"Thomas!" I shrieked. "Don't be so horrible!"

"I wouldn't make anything bad happen to her. Just, like, give her a dose of flu, or something."

"That's disgusting!"

"Why?" said Thomas. "I'm only trying to help."

"Steffi's my friend," I said. "You don't stick pins into your friend!"

"I bet she'd stick them into you fast enough if she was your understudy. You're too soft!" jeered Thomas. "You'll never get anywhere!"

I remembered what Steff was always saying about having to look out for yourself.

Would she stick pins in me?

I tossed my head and said, "You don't know what you're talking about!"

But I wondered if it was true that I was soft, and if so what I could do about it.

Steffi came at four o'clock and we did a bit of practising up in my bedroom – quiet practising, so that Dad couldn't complain – and then Mum called to us that tea was ready. Mum had done a really scrumptious tea! She'd made one of her special chocolate cakes, with icing as deep as a doorstep. On top she'd spelt out the words

Good Luck to you both

in little silver balls. I tucked in and so did Thomas, but Steffi said she was very sorry, she couldn't eat any.

"Not even a tiny little bit?" said Mum. "Not even a taste?"

"Honestly," said Steff, "I couldn't!"

When she'd gone Mum said, "I hope that silly girl isn't on a diet."

She wasn't! Steff loves her food far too much to go on a diet, and anyway, she doesn't need to. She's not fat.

I was really puzzled why she hadn't eaten Mum's chocolate cake.

Chapter 5

On Sunday afternoon as we were having tea, the telephone rang. Mum said, "I'll get it." She went into the hall and I heard her say "Hallo" and then I heard her say "Oh, no!" and "Oh, dear!" and "She must be so disappointed." And then I snatched the last piece of chocolate cake away from Thomas (he'd already gobbled three slices) and after that I didn't really listen any more.

Until Mum came into the kitchen and announced that Steffi was in hospital.

"She's had to have her appendix out, poor little soul. No wonder she didn't feel like any tea yesterday."

The bit of chocolate cake that I was eating suddenly turned into a soggy lump in my mouth.

"She's going to be all right," said Mum, "but of course it means she'll miss the show."

Thomas said, "Blimey, it worked!"

"Thomas, you didn't?" I screamed.

"Didn't what?" said Mum.

"Stick pins in Steffi!"

"It was the power of thought," said Thomas. "Blimey! I never knew you could do things like that."

"Oh, Thomas!" I wailed.

"I should think you should be grateful," said Thomas. "I've given you your big chance!"

Mum said firmly that it was nothing to do with Thomas. "Just coincidence. Stop being so silly!"

Common sense told me that Mum was right. There was no way Thomas could have given Steffi appendicitis! All the same, I still felt dreadful about it. I couldn't help remembering how I'd daydreamed…

"Cheer up!" said Mum. "I know it's horrid for poor Steffi, but there'll be other opportunities. She wouldn't want you to mope."

And of course I didn't mope for very long. I couldn't! It was all too exciting. I was called in for a special rehearsal, just me, by myself, with Buzz Peabody. I was even let off morning classes and sent to the theatre in a cab! It made me feel like a S*T*A*R*.

Buzz Peabody was really amazed that I already knew all the steps for the Rag Doll dance. She told me not to worry that I was a different size and shape from Steff.

"She was one sort of Rag Doll, you're another.

Don't try to be her. You do your own thing."

So I did, and she laughed, and said, "Rag Doll with attitude. I like it!"

On Tuesday we broke up, which meant we could go to rehearsals during the day instead of having to wait till after school. It was like being a real pro! (Pro is short for professional. Something else I'd learnt from Steff.)

We met all the other members of the cast, the grown-up ones, including Richard Dando, who is quite famous. I nearly died when I found myself standing next to him!

Starlotta said, "Of course, I'm used to this sort of thing." Just because her uncle is on telly! He isn't anywhere near as famous as Richard Dando.

Nor as handsome.

Starlotta's uncle looks like a warthog.

On Wednesday, Mum took me to visit Steff in the hospital.

"I'll go and have a cup of tea and leave you two together," she said.

Steff was sitting up in bed looking a bit pale but very pretty. She was wearing this nightdress covered all over in bits of lace and little pink flowers. Almost as good as an evening gown!

I sat on a chair next to the bed and Steff told me all about her appendix. How it had suddenly just burst and how she had been in agony.

I said, "Poor you! You must feel terrible."

"I did," said Steff. "I don't now. I mean, at least I've got it over with. It can't happen twice. Imagine the horror if you'd just landed a big film part, and all of a sudden – OW! OUCH! AGONY!"

Steff did it so well that a nurse came running.

"It's all right," I said, "she's only acting."

The nurse clicked her tongue and said, "You theatricals!"

We giggled at that. But then I grew serious and said, "I feel ever so guilty."

"What about?" said Steff.

"Taking over your part."

"Stevie!" She almost shrieked it at me. And then she remembered that she was in hospital and that hospitals are supposed to be q.u.i.e.t. She clapped a hand to her mouth. "Sorry! But honestly. What d'you feel guilty for? It's not your fault my appendix burst!"

"N-no," I agreed. "I s'ppose not."

"Well, how could it be?"

She didn't know about Thomas.

"Make the most of it," said Steff. "I would!"

It was such a relief to know that we were still friends. There are some people – Starlotta, I bet – who would hate you for ever if you stepped into their shoes. But Steff isn't like that. She really wanted me to do well.

The dress rehearsal went on for ages. Just

everything kept going wrong. The lighting didn't work properly, the costumes didn't fit properly, the scene changes didn't work fast enough, someone even came on in the wrong place!

Dell said, "A bad dress rehearsal means a good performance."

I just hoped she was right.

Next day was Christmas, and Auntie Lily came. She always comes at Christmas. "But this year it's special!" she said, beaming at me.

Auntie Lily was coming to the first night along with Mum and Dad and Thomas. I think she was almost as excited as I was. "We'll all be round afterwards," she promised.

"Round where?" said Thomas. He doesn't know a thing about theatres or theatre people.

"Why, backstage!" cried Auntie Lily. "Where else?"

I got to the theatre in plenty of time to put my make-up on. (I went by cab again – I was getting quite used to it!)

There was the most tremendous hubbub in the dressing room, with everyone chattering as they changed into their costumes. I discovered that there were simply loads of cards waiting for me. Everyone had sent one! Both sets of nans and granddads. Both of our next door neighbours. Auntie Lily. Mum and Dad. Even Thomas! I stuck them round my mirror as I read them.

The last one I opened was from Steff. I couldn't believe what it said!

BREAK A LEG
Love Steff

Break a leg? Oh, and I had really thought that she wanted me to do well! I'd thought we were still friends! How could she say such a thing? She obviously hated me. She wanted me to fail!

I was so upset that I quickly slipped the card into my coat pocket before anyone could see it. How could Steffi be so mean? It wasn't my fault her appendix had burst!

"Hey, Stevie! What's the matter?" Rosa was looking at me quite anxiously in the mirror. "You haven't got stage fright, have you?"

"No!" I scrubbed, fiercely, at my eyes. I hadn't got stage fright. And I wasn't going to let Steffi upset me! She was the one who was always telling us that you had to look out for yourself. You had to be tough to survive. I was going to be the best Rag Doll I possibly could!

It is amazing, really, but the minute you step on stage you forget about absolutely everything except the part you are playing or the steps you are dancing. I didn't think about Steffi and her mean message once! I just danced.

I remembered Buzz Peabody telling me to do my own thing, and so that is what I did. I made my Rag Doll a bit cheeky, a bit perky. People laughed when I tried to do a jump and my sawdusty legs folded up. They laughed when I tried to do a pirouette and my arms went flying about, all out of control. I enjoyed myself! And I got lots and lots of applause!

Richard Dando was waiting in the wings as I came off. He stuck up a thumb and said, "Nice one!" I glowed all the way to the dressing room.

It wasn't until afterwards, when we had all taken our bows and the curtain had come down for the last time, that I remembered about Steff. It made me feel so sad. It took away some of the sparkly feeling and the happiness. Steffi was my friend! How could she be so unkind?

Auntie Lily had arranged for us all to go and have supper after the show. She said you always did that on a first night. In the restaurant I pulled off my coat and Steffi's card slid out. Thomas immediately pounced on it.

"What's this?"

I snatched at it. "Give it here! It's mine!"

"Break a leg?" said Thomas. "What a thing to say! Fancy telling someone to go and break a leg!"

To my surprise, Auntie Lily threw back her head and laughed. She laughed and laughed, and all the other people in the restaurant turned to look at her.

(Auntie Lily has a rather loud sort of laugh.)

"Oh, you funny boy!" she said. "Break a leg doesn't mean *break a leg*!"

"So w-what does it mean?" I said.

"In the theatre it means GOOD LUCK!" roared Auntie Lily.

I knew then that Steffi and me really were friends. We'd be friends for ever!

Sweet Success

Chapter 1

"It's ages since we've been for an audition," grumbled Rosa as we were changing into our leotards one afternoon, ready for Movement Class with Miss Merchant. "Ages and ages...not since Christmas!"

Rosa is one of my friends at the Starlight Stage School. The school is in London and we have a special badge that is stitched on to our leotards and sweat shirts and the bright red cloaks that we wear in winter. Our sworn enemies from the Mona West Academy jeer at our cloaks. They call us the Red Riding Hoods. But we don't care! Cloaks are different, and we're different, too. The Monas wear puke yellow that looks like dog sick.

My other friends besides Rosa are Steffi and Dell. Steffi is my special friend. We are Steffi and Steve. Or sometimes Stevie and Steff. "Like a double act," my brother Thomas says. But we are not at all alike! Steff is pink and pretty and just a teeny tiny weeny little bit plump. Nicely plump! *Cuddly* plump.

I am small and freckled with short brown hair cut sort of raggedy. Mum says it suits me that way as I have a funny cheeky-looking face. "Like a pixie," she says. Prettyish, but not at all beautiful. Dell is the beautiful one! Rosa is what Mum calls "a chirpy Cockney sparrow" and is even smaller than I am. We all go round together in a gang.

I was surprised when Rosa grumbled about us not being sent for auditions.

"Do we expect to be?" I said. I'd only been at Starlight for one term, so I wasn't sure.

"They send the Monas," said Rosa. "They go for auditions all the time."

"Oh, well! That lot." Steffi pulled her long blonde hair back into a scrunchy. "They're only interested in making money."

"I wouldn't mind making money," said Rosa.

"We will," promised Steff. "As soon as we're a bit older. They'll send us for heaps of things when we're older. It doesn't do to start too young. That's what my mum says."

Steffi's mum is an actor, so she ought to know. But Starlotta, of course, couldn't resist boasting. "I was appearing in commercials when I was only two years old. I was in an ad for diapers."

"Pardon me?" said Dell. She cupped a hand to her

ear. "An ad for what, did you say?"

"Diapers," said Starlotta, in lofty tones.

There was a silence, and then I realised what she meant. "Nappies!" I cried. "Diapers is American for nappies!"

Starlotta in a nappy ad! Everyone just collapsed.

"Oh! What did you have to do?" gasped Steff. "Lie there on a table while your mummy changed you?"

"I crawled about," said Starlotta.

That just made us giggle even worse. I fell to my knees and started crawling, and soon all the rest had joined in. We crawled to and fro across the changing room, making baby noises.

"Goo gah gah!" went Steff.

"Boo hoo! I've wet my nappy!" announced Rosa.

It was a bit mean of us, I suppose, but Starlotta asks for it. She is always making like she's so much better than the rest of us. It's probably something to do with having such a stupid name. I mean, Starlotta! I ask you! I bet her mum called her that hoping everyone would shorten it to Star. Nobody ever does, though, 'cos nobody likes her. Only her yucky friend Tiffany, who is so mindless it is just unbelievable.

The bell rang and we all headed for the dance studio, where Miss Merchant was waiting for us. Me and Rosa were still crawling and making baby noises.

Miss Merchant said, "On your feet, you two! We'll start with some voice exercises. Deep breath!

Hold...one, two...slowly, slowly, let it out...slowly, Starlotta...and another one! Hold, one, two—"

"This is so boring," muttered Starlotta.

Well! Voice exercises might not be the most exciting thing we do, but that was a really dumb thing to say. Miss Merchant kind of, like, *frrrrroze*.

"Excuse me?" she said. "You find it...boring, did you say?"

"Well, what I mean–" Starlotta waved a hand, "I just don't see the point of it."

"The point, my dear Starlotta," said Miss Merchant, "is to teach you control of your voice. How to speak without running-out-of-breath. How to **P R O J E C T**!" Miss Merchant suddenly opened up and practically deafened us. "You want to be **HEARD**, don't you? There's nothing worse than sitting in a theatre and not being able to **HEAR**."

Starlotta tossed her head. She actually had the *nerve*. "I'm not going into theatre." Honestly! The things that girl says. "Theatre's way past its sell-by date. I'm only going to do films and television."

Miss Merchant gave a short, amused laugh. "When you're out in the big wide world, my dear, you'll do whatever's offered. Jobs don't exactly hang off trees, you know!"

"My uncle—" began Starlotta, but everyone groaned. Starlotta goes on and on about her uncle. He's this big television star and he looks like a warthog. He is probably quite nice, really, but we all just get sick to death of hearing about him.

Anyway, Miss Merchant said rather crushingly that she didn't wish to know about Starlotta's uncle just at the moment.

"Here in this room I don't care what famous relatives you have. I judge you on what I see, not on who your mum and dad or auntie and uncle happen to be."

Hooray! That put Starlotta in her place. But after class, when the four of us were walking up the road together, Rosa said something that worried me. She said, "It's all very well Miss Merchant saying what she did. Not caring if someone has famous relatives. But it does help if you have one."

She meant Starlotta's gross warthoggy old uncle.

"I mean, it stands to reason," said Rosa, "doesn't it?"

"Yeah." Dell nodded, and her shiny black hair bobbed and bounced. "You've got a famous uncle on the telly, he could get you a part, no problem. Just got to ask."

Dell didn't sound in the least bit bitter, but then Dell never does. She's so beautiful, she doesn't have to. She's not in the least vain about it, no way! But it has given her this massive

C O N F I D E N C E

about a thousand metres high.

I wish I had as much confidence as Dell!

I wish I had an uncle that was on television.

I wish I had a mum and dad that were actors.

All I have is **AMBITION**.

I am going to work as hard as I can and never, ever give up. And in the end I will become a $S*T*A*R*$. But you can't become a star unless you are given the chance to show how brilliant you are. Rosa was right! It was time we were sent to another audition.

Chapter 2

Next day, I could hardly believe it. A group of us were called in to see Miss Todd, our drama teacher, and she told us that we were being sent for – an audition!

Rosa looked at me and giggled, and I giggled back. Miss Todd said, "What is so funny, you girls? Going for auditions is a serious business."

We couldn't really tell her what we were giggling about! Rosa gave a little hiccup and clamped a hand to her mouth. I said, "We're excited!"

Miss Todd smiled. "It is exciting, I agree. We don't expect you all to get parts, but it will do you good to have a go. It's all experience."

She said that the audition was for a TV commercial for a new brand of sweet called Frooties.

"The idea is that they have lots of you dressed up as fruits – strawberries, raspberries, blackberries…all sorts! But remember," said Miss Todd, "auditioning

53

for a commercial is not the same as auditioning for a play. They don't necessarily expect you to act. What they're mainly looking for is faces. So don't be upset if they don't pick you. It just means that on this occasion you weren't the type they were after."

"She only said that to make people feel better," said Starlotta, later. "Anyone who really stands out—" she did a little twirl, "will always be noticed."

"Get her," muttered Rosa.

"She didn't say *she'd* stand out," said Tiffany.

But we all knew that was what she meant. Talk about a blabbermouth!

"You've got to admit," said Steff, "she has some nerve. Just imagine how everyone will jeer if she doesn't get anything!"

Of course, we all hoped like mad that she wouldn't. That girl really got on our nerves!

I think I got on Thomas's nerves when I got home that evening.

"Mum, Mum!" I yelled. "We've got an audition!"

Thomas groaned. "Not again!"

I said, "What d'you mean, not again? The last audition I went to was before Christmas."

"Yes," said Thomas, "and we all had to suffer. Oh, I shall just *die!*" He clasped his hands to his heart. "If I don't get anything, I shall just die!"

"That was different," I said. "That was for a proper show. This is just a commercial."

"Oh, I see." Thomas nodded in that horrid superior way that he has. "Just something vulgar, to make money. Not art."

"It's all experience," I said. "But they're only looking for faces so it won't be my fault if they don't pick me. It'll just mean they don't want my particular sort of face."

"Who would?" jeered Thomas.

Thomas is always doing what he calls "putting me in my place". Squashing me. He says it is necessary to stop me becoming bumptious. Mostly I don't take any notice of him. He's terribly serious-minded. He reckons acting is a frivolous occupation.

Mum wanted to know what the commercial was for, so I told her that it was for Frooties, and that they were going to have people dressed as different kinds of fruits.

"What on earth for?" said Thomas.

I said, "I don't know! How should I know? Maybe they'll want us to do little fruit dances." And I skipped off across the room doing a strawberry dance. Bounce – *squish* – bish – *squash*! Bounce – *squish* –

"She's off again," said Thomas.

"I've got to practise! Look, what's this one?"

Hop – skip – twizzle – *spring*. Hop – skip –

"Brussels sprout," said Thomas.

"Brussels sprout's not a fruit! I'm being a cherry."

Hop – skip –

"I thought you said they only wanted faces?"

"Yes, but I'm getting into the mood. How d'you think a banana would dance?"

"I shouldn't think they'd have a banana," said Mum.

"So what would they have?"

"Mm...peach? Passion fruit?"

"Passion fruit!" I snatched up Sheba, who is one of our cats, and began to cover her in kisses. "Mwah! Mwah! Mwah!" Then I whirled off across the room, clutching her to me. Thomas made a being-sick noise.

"Mum, does she have to?" he said.

Mum just laughed and told him to stop being such a misery.

"Of course," sighed Thomas, "I have to remember that she is still very young."

Huh! You'd think Thomas was about ninety, the way he carries on. He is only a year older than me!

Chapter 3

The audition was held the very next day. We all travelled on the tube to Leicester Square, and Miss Todd came with us. The people who were making the commercial were called Fogel, Fitch & Fairlie Walker, which for some reason made me and Rosa go off into one of our fits of giggles. We kept chanting it as we sat on the tube: "Fogel, *Fitch*, & Fairlie Walker!"

In the end Miss Todd had to tell us to be quiet and stop showing off. She said she was ashamed to be seen with us.

"Just behave yourselves! You'll give the school a bad name."

After that we sat quiet as mice and didn't look at each other. We knew that if we looked we'd only start off giggling again.

"It's so unprofessional," grumbled Starlotta.

Fogel, Fitch (and Fairlie Walker) lived right at the top

of a skyscraper building made of shiny green glass, like something out of a fairy tale. We sailed up to the sixteenth floor in a lift that had mirrors all round it. I couldn't help shooting anxious glances at myself and wondering whether I had the sort of face that they were looking for. Yes, and I wasn't the only one! I caught Starlotta doing it, as well.

The lift glided to a halt and we all trooped out and walked along a corridor covered in thick white carpet. One of the boys jabbed at Rosa and whispered, "Hey, you'd better watch out! This carpet's so thick a little thing like you could get lost in it."

Rosa biffed at him and Miss Todd said, "Ryan, sh! That's enough."

They're very strict at Starlight. They don't like you doing anything that might give the school a bad name.

At the end of the corridor was a glass door with the word RECEPTION printed on it. Miss Todd went through, and we followed. And, oh, help! The room was full of Monas! Dozens of them, sitting there in their yucky yellow uniforms, all smug and self-satisfied 'cos they'd got there first.

One of the Monas was a girl called Daniela that I recognised from the Christmas show we'd been in. She wasn't too bad, for a Mona. She came over to me and Rosa and said, "It's OK, we've already been in. We're just waiting for our teacher."

"What was it like?" said Rosa.

Daniela shrugged. "Oh! You know. Same as always."

Rosa nodded, wisely. I waited till the Monas had gone swaggering off, then whispered, "What did she mean, same as always?"

"No idea," said Rosa.

Rosa is so cool! She wasn't going to let on to a Mona that we'd never been for a commercial before. Whatever you do, you can't afford to let them think they're superior. They already crow quite enough as it is, just because their school is nearer the West End than ours.

While we were waiting to be called, a man came out and took our photographs. I asked if I could have a look at mine, just to make sure I hadn't come out like a squashed toad or a lump of mashed potato, which is the sort of thing that can happen if the camera catches you at the wrong moment. The man didn't seem to mind, but Starlotta rolled her eyes and mouthed, "Un-pro-FESSION-al."

I didn't see why it was unprofessional. If I'd come out like a mashed potato I would have asked him to take another one. But anyway, I looked OK apart from my ears sticking out, but there's nothing I can do about that. I've tried using chewing gum and I've tried using sticky tape and just nothing seems to work. Mum says I'm over-sensitive and that nobody else even notices. But if you want to be a $S*T*A*R*$ you have to be aware of these things.

A woman with long silver fingernails and slinky black trousers checked off our names on a list. One by one we were called in. They were doing it in alphabetical order, and as my surname is Silver it meant I was one of the last to be called. I always am!

Rosa is lucky as she is Rosa Carmirelli. And Dell is Dell Dugard. Even Steff is Steffi McGowran, which isn't too bad. They all went in before me! I just had to sit there and try not to chew my nails, which is a stupid habit that I've got.

Miss Todd wouldn't let anyone say what it was like, or tell what questions they'd been asked. She said that it wouldn't be fair and we all had to wait our turn. So we sat in glum silence, like at the dentist.

"You can talk, you know," said Miss Todd. "I didn't say don't talk! I just said don't discuss."

But nobody could think of anything to talk about. Starlotta, trying to show how terribly professional she was, picked up a magazine and pretended to read it. I knew she was only pretending when I looked over her shoulder and saw that it was all in a foreign language. When they called her name— "Starlotta Sharman?" she gave this little start, making like she had totally forgotten what she was there for.

I almost tore off a whole fingernail while I was waiting for her to come out. I just couldn't help it.

I'd told Thomas that a commercial wasn't the same as a real show, and of course it isn't. But I still most desperately wanted to be picked!

I prayed inside my head, over and over: *please let them be looking for someone like me!* A freckle-faced pixie with sticking-out ears...it didn't seem very likely. But as Steffi is fond of saying, you never know your luck.

Starlotta came back with this big smirking smile on her face. I could just feel her looking at my freckles and my ears and thinking, "She doesn't stand a chance!" But I took a deep breath and went marching in.

The room was absolutely mega-normous. One whole wall was nothing but window! All dotted about were these very low, glass-topped tables and white spindly chairs. Long green trailing things were growing out of pots, and huge monster fans hung from the ceiling like giant spiders. Really creepy!

At the far end of the room there was a man in a red shirt sitting at a table. Behind him there were three more men and a girl in a sparkly top. They were all wearing dark glasses like gangsters in an American movie. The man in the red shirt said, "And who have we here? Stevie, isn't it? Stevie Silver. Hi there, Stevie! I'm Gus. These are Mike, Pete, Andy and Gill...Mike, Pete, Andy, Gill, meet Stevie."

Everyone said "Hi!" so I said "Hi" back. They

laughed when I said it. I don't know why. I was only being polite.

On my way across the room I bumped into a table and got tangled up with one of the trailing things and they all laughed again. I felt really stupid. I bet Starlotta hadn't got tangled in a trailing thing!

Gus said, "OK, Stevie! This is a commercial for Frooties, as I expect you know. Here's the story line."

I did my best to look intelligent

"Boy and girl in sweet shop, gazing at the sweets. Yum yum! Which ones shall they buy? They can't decide! Then all of a sudden – whoosh!" He threw up his hands. "A tube of Frooties bursts open and all the fruits come spilling out...raspberries, strawberries—"

"Oranges, lemons—"

"Blackberries—"

"Mangoes—"

All the others had joined in, excitedly calling out the names of fruits.

"Does that sound fun or does that sound fun?" said the one called Pete.

I said, "That sounds absolutely brilliant," and they all laughed yet again. I couldn't think what I'd said that was amusing. I was just trying to show them that I felt as excited as they did.

"Okey-dokey! Let's get down to business. Mike?"

One of the other men stood up and pointed a video camera at me.

"I want you to look into this camera, Stevie, and shout out the word *Frooties!* Can you do that?"

"I should think so," I said. It didn't sound very difficult.

"You won't dry when the camera starts rolling?"

I said indignantly that of course I wouldn't. I said, "Miss Todd would be furious if any of us did that."

So then they laughed *yet again*. I still couldn't understand why they kept doing it, but I was getting used to it by now. Gus said, "Right. Off you go!"

The camera light came on. I looked straight at it and shouted, "FROOOteeeeze!" as loudly as I could. The girl in the sparkly top said, "Ace!" Mike stuck up a thumb.

"OK, Stevie." Gus leaned across to shake my hand. I blinked. Was that it?

They obviously didn't want me! Something must have put them off. Was it the freckles? Was it the ears? Or was it because I'd got caught in the trailing thing?

"Thanks a bunch! Nice of you to come along."

"Please don't mention it," I said.

It was just good manners. I was just being polite. There wasn't any reason for them to laugh.

Gus picked up the end of his tie and dabbed at his eyes. "Oh, I love it! This one we have to use. Don't worry, Stevie! You'll be hearing from us."

Wow!

WOW!

I reeled back outside and collapsed on a chair next to Steff. I was absolutely bursting to tell someone what Gus had said. *You'll be hearing from us...* Had he said it to everyone? Or just to me?

I couldn't wait to find out!

Chapter 4

As soon as we could, we exchanged notes.

"And then I had to shout *Frooties!*" said Steff, "straight into the camera."

"Yeah." Dell nodded. "Me, too."

"Me, too!" I said.

"Me, too!" said Rosa.

It turned out that everyone had had to shout it.

"He asked *me* if I'd dry when the camera started rolling."

"Yes, he asked me that!"

He'd asked everyone the same question.

"What did you say?"

Steffi giggled. "I said I hoped not!"

"I said Miss Todd would be furious with us if we did anything like that."

"You didn't?" Starlotta spun round, accusingly.

"Yes, I did." I tilted my head. "And he laughed."

"So *unprofessional*," hissed Starlotta.

"Unprofessional," tittered Tiffany.

I turned my back on them and went stalking off ahead with Steff and the others. We were walking to the tube station, a great gaggle of us. We weren't supposed to walk in gaggles. Miss Todd said it cluttered the pavement and gave the school a bad name.

"What did he say right at the end?" I asked Steffi.

"Oh, just...thank you for coming and we'll be in touch."

"That's what they always say!" yelled Starlotta. "It just means they haven't yet made up their minds. They say it to everyone."

"Did he say it to you?" said Steff. "Oy!" She poked at me. "Did he say it to you?"

"N-no. He said—"

"What? What did he say?"

"He said, *This one we have to use*. And then he said, *Don't worry, you'll be hearing from us.*"

There was a stunned silence.

"He said *what*?" said Dell.

"He said, *Don't worry, you'll be hearing from us...*"

"Before that!"

"Before that he said, *This one we have to use.*"

"Jumping Geronimo!"

"You've got a part!" said Steff.

Starlotta, for once, didn't say anything at all.

When I got home I hurled myself into the kitchen shouting, "Mum, Mum, I've got a part!"

"Oh, that's wonderful!" cried Mum. "What part is it?"

"And how much are they paying?" said Thomas.

I had to admit that I hadn't yet been told which part it was. All I knew was that I'd got one!

"But what about the money?" roared Thomas.

Mum said, "Oh, Thomas, as if the money matters! It's the honour and glory."

"Is it?" said Thomas. "I thought it was the money."

"Who cares about money? Not me!"

I went dancing off round the kitchen doing my strawberry dance. Bounce – *squish* – bish – *squash*! I felt sure that I would be picked as a strawberry.

As soon as Dad got in, Mum told him the news. "Stevie's going to be a big star! She's got a part in a commercial!"

"This is excellent," said Dad, rubbing his hands. "If she carries on like this I'll be able to retire!" And then, like Mum, he wanted to know what part it was.

"She doesn't know," said Thomas. "She doesn't even know what they're paying!"

I explained that they had promised I would be hearing from them. I told Dad how Gus had said, "This one we have to use."

"Well, let's hope he's as good as his word," said Dad. "I don't think we ought to start celebrating until it's actually in the bag."

"What bag?" I said.

"He means, until the contract's signed," said Mum.

"Oh!" I wasn't terribly interested in contracts. I just wanted to know what part I'd got!

On the tube next morning with Steffi I said, "I should think I'd be a strawberry, wouldn't you? I have a strawberryish sort of face."

"Well, you said it," said Steff.

I assured her that I didn't mind. "I'd sooner be a strawberry than a raspberry. I don't like raspberries. But of course I'll be whatever they want me to be."

"Don't have much choice, really," muttered Steff.

As we left the tube station we met up with some of the others. Dell and Rosa, Tiffany and Starlotta.

"Well?" said Starlotta. "Have you heard yet?"

"Not yet," I said.

"Oh, I am surprised! I thought they'd have been in touch immediately."

"They wouldn't get in touch with Stevie," said Dell. "They'd ring the school."

"Oh, well! He's probably on the telephone right now." Starlotta turned, with a sweet smile, to Tiffany. "They obviously didn't want anyone too pretty."

"No, 'cos if they had they'd have chosen you," gushed Tiffany.

Ugh! She is so yucky.

"You don't have to get on my case," I said. I did my little strawberry dance along the pavement.

Bounce – *squish* – bish – *squash*. "I can't help it if he gives me a part."

"Stevie, what exactly are you doing?" said Rosa, as I strawberried past her and almost knocked an old lady into the gutter.

"I'm being a strawberry!"

"Ha!" said Starlotta. "So that's what he was looking for!" And she immediately began to copy my strawberry dance, except that she did it with puffed-out cheeks and bent knees and her bottom stuck up in the air. Flump – *bump* - plish – *plosh*. "Squashed strawberry!"

Everyone giggled; even Steff.

I didn't care! They were just jealous. All of them.

"You know what you'll be," I said to Starlotta, "if you get a part...you'll be a *gooseberry!*"

I puckered my mouth as if I was eating lemons and I held my arms very stiff and straight at my sides and did a bright green gooseberry dance right in front of her, all thin and mean and mimsy.

"Sour goosegog!" I cried. "That's what you'll be!"

Later that day Mrs MacPherson, who is the school secretary, came into our classroom and said that Miss Todd wanted to see the following people in her office immediately before lunch: "Della Dugard, Steffi McGowran, Starlotta Sharman and Ricky Robson."

Rosa shot a look at me. I smiled, brightly. I wasn't worried! Gus had promised. "You'll be hearing from us..."

The minute the bell rang, the four of them went dashing off, helter skelter, for Miss Todd's office. They weren't supposed to run in the corridor, but nobody stopped them.

"Well," said Rosa, "it's very odd. If he *promised*."

"It's probably about something quite different," I said.

But oh, it wasn't! When they came back, they were all happy and beaming. They had all got parts in the Frootie ad! Dell was a passion fruit, Steffi was a peach, Ricky was a mango. And Starlotta—

Starlotta was a *strawberry*.

Chapter 5

Just for a minute, I felt I was going to be sick all over the lunch table. My tummy ballooned right up into my mouth, my hands went all wet and sticky, and my knife and fork started to shake and make tinkly noises on my plate.

And then Steffi said, "By the way, Miss Todd wants to see you as soon as you've finished lunch."

"About what?" I said, twiddling my fork in my pasta and trying to make like I couldn't have cared less.

"I don't know, she didn't say. She just said to tell you."

"Oh! Well, I'm going to finish my lunch first," I said.

"That's what she said," said Steff. "There isn't any hurry."

"It's obviously nothing important," I said.

All the same, there was one little bit of me that couldn't help hoping... Maybe they had rung about me specially, and that was why she wanted to see me on my own.

"We were extremely impressed with little Stevie Silver!"

I forced myself to eat my plate of pasta, even though it kept clogging up my mouth so I could hardly swallow it. I even ate my yoghurt, which I had chosen on purpose because it was strawberry. I hoped nobody would notice, but of course old beady-eyed Tiffany did.

"Oh, look, Star!" She pointed. "She's eating your yoghurt!"

I felt like throwing it at her.

As soon as I'd finished I raced off to Miss Todd's office. One of the teachers saw me and yelled, "Stevie Silver! You know you're not supposed to be running in the corridor!" Nobody had told the others not to run.

Miss Todd was waiting for me. She smiled as I came in, but it wasn't the sort of smile that meant she was going to give me good news. It was more of a – a *kind* sort of smile. A try-to-be-ever-so-brave sort of smile.

I found that I'd started shaking again. Miss Todd said, "Sit down, Stevie!"

I sat very quickly, before my legs could give way.

"I'm so sorry," said Miss Todd, "that you weren't offered a part in the Frootie commercial."

It was just as well she'd told me to sit down or I would probably have gone crashing to the floor. I couldn't believe it. I just couldn't believe it! He had *promised*.

Gently, Miss Todd said, "You were so sure you were going to get something, weren't you?"

"He promised me!" I cried. "He said he was going to use me!"

"Oh, Stevie." Miss Todd shook her head. "People say a lot of things."

"You mean, he – he didn't mean it?"

"He probably meant it when he said it. While you were there, in front of him. But then afterwards perhaps he thought about it, or he saw someone else, or things just didn't quite work out the way they were supposed to... I'm afraid, in this business, it doesn't do to count your chickens before they're hatched."

It was what Dad had said. "I don't think we ought to start celebrating until it's actually in the bag."

I dragged the sleeve of my sweatshirt across my eyes. I wasn't going to cry! You had to be tough if you wanted to get anywhere.

"It's a hard lesson," said Miss Todd, "but it's one we all have to learn."

The worst bit was having to go back and face the others. After all the fuss I'd made! Dancing my stupid strawberry dance. Telling Starlotta she was a sour

73

gooseberry. How she would gloat!

She did.

"So much for squashed strawberries," she said.

"And sour gooseberries," said Tiffany, with a little smirk.

"Fancy believing that they meant it!" Starlotta gave an amused trill. "I learnt not to do that when I was about two years old!"

"Stevie doesn't come from a theatrical family," said Tiffany.

"No, that's true." Starlotta stopped trilling and heaved a big sigh, making like she felt just sooo sorry for me. "Poor Stevie! She's got a lot to learn."

I now know how an insect feels when someone treads on it.

FLattenED

I couldn't even think of anything smart to say in reply.

"You don't want to let her get to you," said Steff, as she dragged me away. "She's not worth bothering with! She's garbage."

"Yes, and she can't act to save her life," I muttered.

"Well, she *can*, actually," said Steff. She said it apologetically, but she still said it. "She is quite good, and she has done more work than any of the rest of us."

"That doesn't give her the right to gloat!"

"No, but she's that sort of person. And if you don't mind me saying so," said Steff, "you did rather ask for it...all that showing off in the street!"

I opened my mouth to say that I hadn't been showing off, I'd just been excited. But then I closed it again, because I knew that really and truly Steff was right. I had been excited – but I'd been showing off, as well. I'd been gloating over Starlotta.

I thought when I got home and broke the news that Thomas would gloat over *me*, but to my surprise he didn't. He was quite kind. He even tried to cheer me up.

"After all, it was only a stinky commercial," he said. "Not a proper show."

"That's right," said Mum. "Not worth shedding any tears over."

But I did shed tears, all the same. Only I waited till I was in bed and shed them into my pillow.

There is such a thing as pride.

Chapter 6

I didn't want to go to school next morning. I tried telling Mum I was feeling sick, but she didn't believe me. She said, "Stevie, sweetheart, I know this is hard for you, but you can't just run away from things. You have to face up to them. Be brave! I'm sure it won't be anywhere near as bad as you think."

Mum didn't know Starlotta. She and Tiffany were still going to be gloating, and even some of the others might look at me and think, "Serves her right." I hadn't been boastful – I didn't *think* I'd been boastful – but I could see that maybe I might have got on people's nerves a bit with my strawberry dance.

Me and Steffi travelled to school together on the tube, the same as always. But instead of giggling and gossiping, which is what we usually do, we were quite solemn and serious.

"You mustn't let things get to you," said Steff. "It

happens to everybody at one time or another."

"What, people saying they're going to use you and then not doing it?"

"Yes! Mum says if she could have 10p for every time she's been let down, she'd be a millionaire by now."

"I don't think people should be allowed to say things they don't mean," I muttered.

"Mum says you get used to it. She says you have to learn to take everything with a pinch of salt. It's a tough business," said Steff. She meant show business. "You have to be strong to survive."

I was strong! But it was just so unfair. I said so to Steffi, and she rolled her eyes and said, "Tell me about it!"

In the corridor at school we bumped into Starlotta. She said, "Oh, there you are, Stevie Silver! You're in for it. Miss Todd's looking for you."

"For me?" I said.

"Well, your name is Stevie Silver, isn't it? She wants you in her office straight away. She looks grim! I reckon someone's gone and reported you."

"Reported her for what?" said Steff.

"Giving the school a bad name! Dancing in the street."

"You were doing it, too!" I said.

"I didn't knock an old lady into the gutter."

"Oh!" Steff clapped a hand to her mouth. She

looked at me in dismay. Giving the school a bad name is one of the worst crimes. But knocking an old lady into the gutter...

I swallowed, rather hard.

"You didn't even apologise to her," said Starlotta. "You were too busy showing off."

Steffi gave me a little shove. "You'd better go and get it over with. I'll keep my fingers crossed for you!"

I snailed along to Miss Todd's office and scratched nervously at the door. My heart was banging and thudding. What was she going to say to me?

"Stevie Silver, you are a disgrace to the school!"

She might even expel me.

"Come in!" called Miss Todd.

I eased open the door just the tiniest little crack and sidled through it sideways. I thought perhaps if I was very meek and humble she might forgive me.

"Ah, Stevie!" said Miss Todd. She didn't *sound* grim. She didn't look grim. She was smiling! A proper smile. A happy smile!

"Take a seat, Stevie. Good news! Fogel, Fitch just rang. They want you, after all."

I got as far as "W—" and then my mouth just dropped into this great big O.

"Apparently," said Miss Todd, "they saw you first, and then they saw another girl. It was between the two of you! They couldn't make up their minds. It's taken them all this time! They rang through just this morning to say they wanted you. And it's not to dress up as a Frootie, it's to play a real part – the girl in the sweet shop! Isn't that lovely?"

I tried desperately to change my lips into a different shape so that I could say something, but they seemed to have got permanently stuck into an O shape.

"It means you actually have a speaking part," said Miss Todd. "You get to say—"

My mouth suddenly sprang back into working order.

"FROOOOOteeeeeeze!" I cried.

"Ye-e-es…" Miss Todd pressed both hands to her ears. "I'm glad you've already learnt your lines!"

The others were all in the classroom waiting for registration. Steffi looked at me, anxiously.

"What happened?"

I felt like jumping on to a desk and shouting, "I've got a part! I've got a speaking part!"

But I didn't. I just said in a perfectly ordinary, quiet sort of voice that the advertising agency had rung. "They want me, after all."

"Oh, Stevie! That is brilliant!"

Steffi is so lovely. She came flying over and gave me a huge bear hug.

Starlotta said, "What do they want you for? An orange pip?"

Tiffany snickered. She thought that was really funny.

"No, I'm going to be the girl in the sweet shop," I said.

"Jumping Geronimo!" said Dell. Steffi went into a mock faint. "That's a lead part!"

"Just think...you'll be rich," said Rosa. "You'll earn a fortune!"

I said, "It won't be a fortune. Not like winning the lottery."

"Better than a poke in the eye with a burnt stick," said Rosa.

I felt terrible. I'd been so busy feeling sorry for myself that I'd never bothered to think of poor Rosa. She hadn't been offered anything at all!

"It's only a commercial," I said. "Not like a proper show. It's not going to make me a star overnight."

"Hardly!" brayed Starlotta.

"It's the product that counts," agreed Tiffany. She nodded, wisely. "It's what Starlotta said...they obviously didn't want anyone too pretty. If they had someone too pretty, it would draw attention away from the product."

The product was the most important thing in any commercial. I knew that! I knew that it was Frooties that were important, and not me.

But Steffi said loyally that when people watched it, it would be my face that they remembered.

"You'll be recognised every time you walk down the street."

I'd be the Girl in the Frooties ad!

Saves the Day

Chapter 1

Me and my best friend Steff were talking on the phone.

"Shall I tell you who was really good?" said Steff. "Really, *really* good?"

We were discussing the dress rehearsal of a play that was being put on by the senior pupils at Starlight, which is our stage school. All of us juniors had been allowed to go and watch.

"That girl with the red hair," said Steff. "Millie Murphy. She was *really* good."

"She was," I agreed. "She was absolutely brilliant!"

Somewhere near my left ear I heard this disgusting noise, like a person being sick. It was my brother Thomas, pretending to throw up. I turned my back on him.

"The way she did that bit where she had to fall down the stairs," said Steff.

"I know!" I said. "I nearly *died* !"

"I really thought she'd gone and slipped."

"Me, too! I couldn't *believe* it."

Thomas had come dancing round to the front of me. He stood there, pulling stupid faces and making hurry up movements with his hands. I did my best to ignore him.

"They say," said Steff, "that lots of top agents and directors are coming to the performance."

"*No?*" I shrieked.

"It's what I heard," said Steff.

Thomas swooshed at me with his hands. I knew he wanted me to get off the phone, but why should I? I had as much right to talk to people as he did. He could wait!

"Imagine," sighed Steff, "if one of them saw us selling programmes and said, 'That's the girl I want for my next big Hollywood movie'."

"Oh, *wow*!" I did a mock swoon, with the telephone pressed against my forehead. Thomas instantly made a swipe at it, but I kicked at him and he backed off. "I'm fainting just at the thought of it!"

"You're what?" squeaked Steff.

I clamped the telephone back to my ear. "I'm f-f-f-fainting!"

"STUPID LUVVIES!" roared Thomas.

Steffi giggled. "What was that?"

"Only my idiotic brother," I said.

Thomas gave me this really *filthy* look and went

stamping out of the room, slamming the door behind him.

"What's his problem?" said Steff.

"I don't know. Just because he wants to use the telephone, I expect. He's one big pain, he—" I broke off as the door banged back open and Thomas reappeared. He had Mum with him.

"Uh-oh!" I said. "The heavy mob!"

"Stevie!" Mum pointed crossly at her watch. "Get off the telephone!"

"Gotta go," I said. "Chow!"

Chow was what we were saying that term; I don't know why. Maybe next term it would be 'Afghan hound' or 'Yorkie'. We go through these phases.

"Luvvy!" hissed Thomas.

"Bore," I said.

"Just be quiet," said Mum. "You've been on that phone for nearly three quarters of an hour! What's the matter with your mobile?"

"What's the matter with *his*?" I said.

"It was *stolen*," said Thomas, "if you want to know."

"Well, mine needs re-charging, so there!"

"Not surprised," muttered Thomas, "the amount you talk. It's nothing but stupid luvvy gossip, anyway." He snatched up the phone. "What I have to discuss is *important*."

"Why?" I said. "Who are you ringing? The Prime Minister?"

"Stevie." Mum took my arm and moved me off towards the door. "Leave Thomas alone. He wants to talk to Sam. It's serious."

Serious. Huh! Sam Alexander is this itty squitty boy in Thomas's class at school. He's also Thomas's best friend, like Steffi is mine.

"Have they had a fight?" I said. Me and Steff never have fights. Other people do, but not us. On the other hand, if I was Thomas's friend I would probably have fights with him all the time, practically. He is the most *infuriating* person.

"I suppose they've fallen out," I said.

Mum said no, they hadn't fallen out, but it was something very important.

"It's important what me and Steff were talking about," I said. "We were saying what we thought of the show. *That's* important, if I'm going to be an actor."

Which I am!

✱ ✱ ✱ ✱ ✱ ✱ ✱ ✱ ✱ ✱ ✱

STEVIE SILVER

✱ ✱ ✱ ✱ STAR OF ✱ ✱ ✱ ✱

STAGE AND SCREEN

✱ ✱ ✱ ✱ ✱ ✱ ✱ ✱ ✱ ✱ ✱

That's what I'm going to be.

"We have to develop our critical faculties," I said.

"Yes, I'm sure," agreed Mum, pushing me into the kitchen. "But Thomas is worried about the cats."

"*Our* cats?" I said. "What's wrong with them?"

They were sitting on the table in two furry heaps. A black heap (Sheba) and a fat heap (Bunter). They looked OK to me. Mum explained that it wasn't our cats, it was the cats at Cats' Cottage.

"Oh!" I began to understand. Cats' Cottage is a cat sanctuary run by Sam's mum. It's where our two came from. Thomas helps out there as much as he can. He's crazy about cats. We all are, in our family, but Thomas especially. He's going to be a vet when he grows up. (He's amazingly clever, I have to admit it.)

"They're not short of money again?" I said.

"I'm afraid they are," said Mum. "And this time, it's serious. They might even have to close."

"But what about the cats?" I said.

There are dozens of cats at Cats' Cottage. Big cats, small cats, sick cats, healthy cats. Cats of all kinds. Some of them are blind, or deaf, or have only three legs because of accidents. Some of them have been ill-treated or abandoned. Some are just old. Sam's mum takes them all.

"But where would they go?" I wailed.

"Well, that's the problem," said Mum. "There's a real fear they'd have to be put down."

I stared at her in horror. Put down all those poor

trusting moggies? That would be like murder!

"Now you can see why Thomas is so upset," said Mum.

I was upset, too! Why hadn't someone told me?

Thomas came back into the kitchen. He picked up Sheba and buried his face in her fur.

"So what's happening?" said Mum.

"Got one more week."

"For what?" I said.

"For raising money!" shouted Thomas.

"You don't have to *yell*," I told him. "Why didn't you say anything?"

"What's the point? All you're interested in is your stupid acting! It's all you ever talk about."

"Hush, now," said Mum. "Getting cross isn't going to solve anything."

"That's *right*," I said. "We have to think about the cats."

"I've been thinking about them!" roared Thomas. "While you've been messing around *acting*, I've been doing things!"

"What sort of things?" I said. "Jumble sales? Car boot sales?"

"We've done all that!"

"They've really been trying," said Mum. "You've got another jumble sale tomorrow, haven't you, Thomas?"

Thomas nodded.

"And a big fair in St Andrew's hall next Saturday.

They're doing as much as they possibly can."

"Would you like me to help?" I said.

I said it really politely. Really *graciously*. He was lucky I said it at all, considering how horrid he'd been. But I was thinking of the cats.

"If there's anything I can do, just let me know," I said.

"You?" said Thomas. "What could you do?" He rushed to the door. "Stupid luvvy!"

Mum said I had to forgive him because he was upset, but I made a vow it was the last time *I* would offer to help.

Chapter 2

Next day was Saturday. We don't usually go in to school on a Saturday; just sometimes, like if we have a special rehearsal. But today was when the Upper School were putting on their show, and some of us had been chosen to be ushers.

Being an usher is quite important. It means saying hello to people when they arrive, and offering to take their coats, and asking them if they'd like a programme, and showing them to their seats.

Miss Todd, who is Head of Theatre Studies, told us that we were "representing the school".

"So I want your best manners, please! A smile at all times. You are there to make people feel welcome."

I would like to say that I had been chosen because I was Especially Promising. I mean, I am especially promising. You bet! I am going to be a S*T*A*R*. (This is not boasting: it is my aim in life.)

But in fact all that happened was that Miss Todd put everyone's name in a box and the first six she picked were the ones that got to be ushers. So it was just luck, really.

But as Steffi says, you need a bit of luck if you are going to get anywhere.

"There are some people that are lucky and some that aren't. It's as simple as that."

Our two special friends, Dell and Rosa, had not been lucky. They were dead envious of me and Steff, but not jealous, because of being our friends.

"Friends don't get jealous," said Rosa. "They just want to scratch your eyes out!" And she made scratching motions with her fingers, but we knew she was only joking.

We had to be in school by two o'clock. Miss Todd said that we were to wear school uniform, which was a pity as it meant I couldn't get dressed up and impress agents. I said this to Mum and she laughed and said, "Which agents?"

"Agents that might be there to watch the show," I told her.

"What makes you think they'd be impressed? They're not there to look at you!"

I said, "*Mum*! They might catch sight of me and get me a part in a Hollywood movie!"

"What as?" said Thomas. "A tomato?"

Stupid smart mouth! He only said it because of

our school uniforms being bright red.

"You wait till I'm a big star," I said. "I'll be able to give huge megabuck cheques to people like Sam's mum to help the cats!"

"Be too late by then," muttered Thomas. He choked. "They'll all have been killed!"

"Oh, Thomas!" Mum went chasing after him. "Don't be like that! You've got your jumble sale this afternoon, you've got the fair next weekend... Everyone's doing their very best!"

Everyone except me. I wasn't doing anything. But I'd offered! I wasn't going to offer again.

I flounced upstairs to the bathroom to wash my hair with some special Gleem shampoo that I'd bought. Even in school uniform and looking like a tomato I *might* just be noticed. You never know your luck!

Thomas was leaving the house at the same time as me. He was going down the road to Sam's: I was going up the road to the tube station, to meet Steff. We collided with each other at the front door.

"After you," I said.

"After *you*," said Thomas; and he made this grand gesture like he was Sir Walter Raleigh laying down his cloak for Queen Elizabeth. "You're the big star," he said, "after all."

"Oh, get on, the pair of you!" said Dad. He'd heard from Mum the way we'd been pecking at each other.

"Yes, you'd better shift," said Thomas, "or all the

92

other luvvies will get there first and be spotted before you are."

"Thomas! Button it," said Dad.

At least Dad is on my side. *Sometimes.*

Mum came to see us off. To Thomas she said, "Good luck!" To me she just said, "Have fun!" She didn't take it seriously, the idea that I could end up in a Hollywood movie.

The other people who were ushers were:

Ricky Robson, who has a head like a turnip but is funny

Buster Wells, who is going to grow into a heart throb (my Auntie Lily says so)

Starlotta Sharman, who is one big pain, and

Petal Lovejoy, who is probably going to go bald if she doesn't stop messing with her hair and dyeing it in different colours. (It was all pink and frizzy like candyfloss just at the moment.)

We all gathered in the Green Room, which is like a sort of actors' lounge, waiting for Miss Todd to come and inspect us and dish out some programmes.

"Hey, Stevie! Tell them what your brother called you," said Steff.

"He called me a stupid luvvy," I said. "He's always doing it. He thinks actors are just fribbles."

"I'd like to meet your brother," said Buster.

"No, you wouldn't," I said. "You'd end up wanting to bash him."

"It must be *soo* difficult for you," gushed Starlotta. "I mean, coming from a family without any theatrical connections. I'm so lucky that way!"

Starlotta has this gross fat uncle that's on television. He's OK, really, I guess; it's just that we get bored to death hearing about him all the time. Anyway, I do have theatrical connections. I have my Auntie Lily. I said so to Starlotta.

"Oh, but yes! Of course." Starlotta smiled one of her sickly smiles. "Your Auntie Lily! I was forgetting Auntie Lily. She used to be a pupil here, didn't she? Way back in...when was it? Half a century ago? She must have been here when the school first opened!"

I felt my cheeks growing red and angry. I hate it when people make fun of Auntie Lily. She is Mum's cousin and a bit – well – peculiar, I suppose. Like she wears these really odd clothes that she gets from charity shops. (She once turned up in a dress made of *feathers*!) And she keeps her money in her knickers so that nobody can steal it. She is also quite old. But not as old as all that!

"Did your Auntie Lily ever actually do anything?" said Petal.

"Yes," I said. "She was leading lady with the Penzance Players."

There was a silence.

"Where's Penzance?" said Ricky.

"Cornwall!" I snapped. Dumb stupid turnip head.

"Cornwall." Starlotta nodded, kindly. "Well, I suppose everyone has to start somewhere. Personally I'm going straight into television."

"Oh, really?" I said. "I'm going to go into films."

I looked at myself in the Green Room mirror. I have what Mum describes as a cheeky sort of face. I could play one of those parts where a child is kidnapped by a criminal and they go off together and the child gives the criminal what for and keeps telling him off and bossing him and in the end they become good friends and we discover the criminal isn't so bad after all. That is the sort of part I'd be good at. I wouldn't want to play anything sloppy and slurpy.

"Hey!" said Steff. "I only just noticed...you've washed your hair in something. It's all gleaming!"

"That's because I washed it in GLEEM. Gleem shampoo for really *gleeeeeeeemy* hair," I said, pretending to be someone in a TV commercial. "I did it in case there's any film directors around."

"Film directors!" Starlotta gave an amused titter. "Film directors don't come to drama schools!"

"Well, then, agents," I said.

"Agents only come to the evening performance," said Starlotta.

Me and Steff exchanged glances. Steff pulled

a face. We wouldn't be there in the evening. The older ones were on duty then.

Bother, I thought. I'd gone and wasted money on special shampoo all for nothing!

"I shall probably meet an agent or two," said Starlotta. She did a little twirl. "I'm coming with my uncle. He knows all the top people. He's promised to introduce me."

You see what I mean about Starlotta being a pain. Not just a pain, but a PAIN. One great big enormous megahuge

PAIN

Sometimes I feel like strangling her.

I prayed that Thomas wouldn't ask me if I'd been spotted by anyone. I'd had enough sneering and jeering from Starlotta; I didn't want him starting in on me as well. When I got home, however, I found the house sunk in deepest gloom.

"How did your jumble sale go?" I said brightly to Thomas. I just wanted to show him that I was interested and that I cared. "Did you make oodles of beautiful dosh?"

By way of reply Thomas snarled, "What's it to you?" and went banging out of the room. He was doing a lot of banging and barging just lately. *And* slamming of doors. Usually if we slam doors Mum tells us off. Well, she tells me off. She didn't say a word to Thomas.

"What happened?" I said.

Mum sighed. "I'm afraid it was a disaster. Hardly anybody turned up. They only made about fifty pounds."

"Isn't that enough?" I said. It seemed quite a lot to me, but Mum shook her head.

"Nowhere near! They've got a vet's bill of two hundred. It's such a shame! Thomas and Sam worked so hard."

I couldn't help feeling sorry for Thomas – I mean, he was still my brother even if he had been mean to me – but I felt even more sorry for all the poor cats.

What was going to happen to them? I just couldn't bear to think of it!

Chapter 3

In the middle of the night I woke up with this incredibly and utterly amazingly brilliant idea. Even though I say it myself. It was a WINNER!

I was so excited I wanted to go bouncing out of bed straight away to call Steffi, only I looked at my clock and it said half-past four and I thought maybe Steffi's mum and dad mightn't like me ringing at half-past four. Steffi wouldn't mind. Not when she heard my idea! But parents are strange.

I once woke my mum and dad to tell them something Miss Todd had said to me at school. She'd said I had the makings of a real comedian. "I can see you with your own television show one of these days!"

Well! I mean. You'd think any normal parents would instantly go whizzing downstairs for a bottle of champagne. A daughter with her own television show! Instead, Dad just groaned and Mum said, "Why are

you telling us this at one o'clock in the morning?"
I said, "Because you've both been out all evening and
I fell asleep and then I woke up and wanted you to
know!" But they didn't want to know. They just wanted
to go to sleep.

So I didn't ring Steff. I lay there with this brilliant
idea fizzing round my brain and lots of other, littler
ideas going off like firecrackers. Whoosh! Swish!
Bang! I was glad when morning came, I can tell you.
I had to ring Steffi straight away! Unfortunately my
mobile seemed to have gone dead. It is always doing
that and it isn't 'cos I talk too much, it's because
I need a new one. I asked Dad if I could borrow his.

"I need to have a private conversation."

"You think anyone wants to listen to the stuff you
yatter on about?" jeered Thomas.

"You did the other day," I said.

"I did not," said Thomas.

"You did so!"

"I did not!"

"You did s—"

"Oh, for heaven's sake!" said Dad. "Here! Take the
phone and go and shriek in your bedroom and give us
all some peace."

Thomas smirked. "Two little luvvies having
secrets," he said.

I almost felt like giving the phone back to Dad and
saying, "If that's how you feel, I won't bother!" But my

99

idea was just so brilliant. And, anyway, it was for the cats. Not for Thomas.

Steff agreed with me that my idea was brilliant. She said that I was a genius to have thought of it.

"Except that a week doesn't give us very much time," she said.

I said that was why I had rung her. "So we can get started."

"What, you mean like today?" said Steff.

"Like *immediately*," I said.

"OK. So who do you reckon we should use?"

"Everybody that's willing!"

"Everybody in our class? Even Starlotta?"

I struggled for a moment then said, "Yes. Even Starlotta." Starlotta's a pain but she is quite a good actress and has had lots of experience. Also, I reminded myself again, it was for the *cats*.

"What about boys?" said Steff.

I struggled a bit more. The trouble with boys is that they tend to take over. They talk in loud voices and won't let anyone else get a word in. And then, before you know it, they're in charge and telling everyone what to do. I don't think they mean to. It's just something they can't seem to help. But this was my idea and I didn't want anyone taking over.

"Maybe the boys won't want to," I said. "But if they do – I suppose we'll have to let them."

I am not sexist. No way! I just don't like being

100

pushed around. But Ricky and Buster aren't too bad; and it was for the cats.

Steffi and me talked for nearly an hour, then her mum yelled at her that her nan had arrived and she had to go.

"See you tomorrow," she said. "We'll get people organised."

After Steff had gone, I rang Rosa. When Rosa heard my idea she said, "Oh! A sort of musical."

"Sort of," I said.

"Like *Cats*."

"It's *for* cats," I said. "To stop them being killed."

"I meant the show called *Cats*. Have you seen it?"

And then she starts off warbling at the other end of the line, because Rosa loves to sing. It's her great passion in life. She's only tiny but she has this immensely enormous voice that can break glasses and make the floor shake. Once she starts you just can't stop her.

I stood there with Dad's mobile held at arm's length, waiting for the noise to die down. It's a bit shattering when it's going straight into your ear.

"We could do some numbers from it!" carolled Rosa, getting all excited.

"No," I said. "This is going to be *our* show. Not one written by other people."

"Oh." Rosa sounded disappointed. "How can we write a musical in one week?"

I said, "We're not going to write a musical! It's a *happening*."

"But don't I get to sing?" said Rosa anxiously.

"Only catty songs…miaaaaaaaow!" I yowled at her down the telephone. Bunter, who was curled up on my bed, stared at me in catty outrage. Maybe it was because I'd interrupted his sleep. Or maybe I was saying something rude in catty language. Rosa heaved a sigh.

"You won't be getting the best out of me. I have to sing if I'm really going to come alive."

"You could always miaow a tune," I said. And I started making cat sounds to the tune of '*Old MacDonald had a Farm*'.

"mee ow,
mee ow,
mee ow"

"Stop!" shrieked Rosa. "That's terrible!"

It's true that singing is not my strongest point. When I am a star with my own show I shall sing funny songs and make people laugh.

"Do some thinking," I told Rosa, and she promised that she would.

Next I rang Dell. Dell is always very cool. She never gets stage fright, she never bawls or yells. She listened while my big idea, plus all the littler ones, came tumbling out, and then at the end she said, "Hm! Looks like we shall have to get started straight away."

"Do you really think we can do it?" I asked Dell.

"Do anything if you put your mind to it," said Dell.

I began to feel a whole lot happier when Dell said that. After talking to Rosa I'd almost begun to get cold feet. Suppose everybody just wanted to do their own thing and nobody would co-operate and we all just ended up arguing? Then we'd really be like silly luvvies and I would feel so ashamed. All those poor darling cats would be killed and I wouldn't have done a thing to help save them.

I'd been talking to Dell for about half an hour when there was a rat-a-tat-tat on my bedroom door. I thought it was Thomas coming for Bunter so I yelled, "Go away! I'm having a private conversation here!"

It wasn't Thomas. It was Dad. He opened the door and stuck his head round and said, "Stone me! You're not still on that phone?"

I didn't dare make any jokes about the heavy mob. Dad was definitely not looking pleased.

"I'd better go," I said to Dell.

"Yes, I think you had," said Dad. He held out a hand for the telephone. "That's the last time I trust you with this, young lady! You brought this phone up here over two hours ago!"

"I haven't been talking *all* the time," I said.

"No? Well, we shall see," said Dad, "when the bill comes in."

He went on and on. You'd think I'd committed some truly hideous crime. All I'd been doing was just trying to save some little cats' lives!

We sat down to dinner and Dad was still going on. Grumbling to Mum about the cost of telephone bills.

"Goodness knows who she's been calling! New York, Sydney—"

"I don't know anyone in New York," I said. "And I don't know anyone called Sidney."

"All right, miss! That's enough smart mouth," said Dad.

I looked at him, hurt. What had I said?

"Stupid luvvy!" jeered Thomas.

I was going to kick him under the table, but I reminded myself just in time that he was upset about the cats. So I glared at him instead.

If he hadn't been so horrid to me I'd have told him about my brilliant idea and stopped him worrying. As it was, he would just have to *wait* !

Chapter 4

Next day at break time, me and Steff gathered all our class together in the corner of the playground and told them my idea for saving the cats of Cats' Cottage. Everyone except Starlotta agreed that it was brilliant.

Starlotta just stood there pulling faces and rolling her eyes and making like she was *sooo* superior. Like she thought my idea was really stupid and babyish and she didn't want anything to do with it. So I ignored her. She hates being ignored.

"First we've got to find out who wants to be in and who doesn't," I said.

"Hands up everyone who does," ordered Steff.

All the girls put their hands up. Even, in the end, Starlotta. She heaved this big dramatic sigh and said, "Oh, I *suppose*…if it's for *cats*," and sort of drooped her arm over her head.

"Is that meant to be up or down?" said Steff.

"Up!" snapped Starlotta.

She just couldn't bear to be left out.

Only two of the boys said they could do it, Ricky and Ahmed Khan. All the rest were playing football on Saturday afternoon. I was secretly a bit relieved about this, though naturally I didn't say so.

"Now we've got to decide who's going to be the lady who rescues the cats," I said.

Nobody wanted to be the lady who rescued the cats because everybody wanted to be cats. Rosa said that the tallest person should do it, and we all agreed. But we had *two* tallest people, Dell and Starlotta. It wasn't until we stood them back to back that we discovered Dell was taller than Starlotta by about a quarter of a millimetre. Starlotta immediately said that meant that Dell had to be the lady.

Steff then pointed out that Dell really *had* to be a cat, because Dell looks like a cat, and this is perfectly true. Dell has this beautiful cat-shaped face with big wide-apart eyes and little catlike nose. Starlotta has a *long* nose and a *long* face. She doesn't look in the least like a cat.

We wasted simply ages arguing about this, until at last I had another of my totally brilliant ideas – I am full of them! – and pointed out to Starlotta that the lady who rescued the cats would be the STAR PART.

I said, "You'll be the one who asks people for money."

So then she changed her mind and said OK, in that case she supposed she'd better do it. Making like she was the only one that possibly *could*, being so much better than the rest of us. But I didn't mind, if it kept her happy. I was just thinking of the cats!

"Now what do we do?" said Petal.

I said, "Now we have to decide what sort of cats we're going to be."

"I'm going to be a tom cat!" shouted Ricky. "Big fierce tom cat!"

Ahmed said that he was going to be a tom cat, too. Being a tom cat meant having punch-ups and chasing all the lady cats.

"Like this!"

Before I knew it, everyone was rushing about screaming and yowling and making catty sounds. When I say everyone, I mean – well! I mean that I was doing it, too. This is the sort of thing that happens when you have boys around. Everything gets all mad and noisy.

Suddenly, in this really loud, cross voice, Starlotta demanded, "Are we trying to save cats or are we just playing stupid games?"

"We're chasing women!" bawled Ricky. He made a lunge at Rosa. Rosa screeched and fell over. Ricky fell on top of her. Rosa giggled.

"You are all so *unprofessional*!" yelled Starlotta.

It was that that made us stop. I felt really ashamed. We were pupils at a famous stage school! We were supposed to be *serious*. Plus we had all those poor moggies depending on us to save them from a horrible death.

"Behaving like a bunch of five-year-olds," grumbled Starlotta. "If we're going to do this thing, then let's do it!"

Even Starlotta has her good points.

All that week we worked on my idea. We told Miss Todd what we were planning and she said we could use the gym for rehearsing in.

Everyone made up their own little cat story and their own little cat character to go with it. We were going to tell the stories just with dance steps and mime, except for Rosa who said she was going to sing a little kitty song, but that was all right. Rosa can sing in tune even without any music.

We all practised our cat make-up and made our own cats' tails to pin to the backs of our leotards. It's easy making a cat's tail! You just take a pair of old tights and cut off one leg and stuff it with something soft, like cotton wool. Then if you wriggle your bottom it swishes about just like a real tail!

Dell had a clever idea how to make paws. She took another pair of tights and cut off the feet part. Then she sewed bits of tape on to them – the feet part,

I mean – and put her hands inside and tied the tapes round her wrists, and there she was, with cats' paws! Cats' mittens, Rosa said they were. From a distance it looked really good, especially when she did catty sort of things such as rubbing her whiskers or washing behind her ears. Of course, the boys said they couldn't do it.

"Can't sew," said Ahmed.

"Then it's time you learnt!" snapped Rosa.

"But it's girls' stuff," said Ricky.

"So's this!" cried Rosa; and she took hold of him by both his ears and stuck out her tongue. In the end they said they'd get their mums to do it. Pathetic!

Friday lunch time we held a dress rehearsal in the gym. Miss Todd asked if she could come and watch, so we were all on our best behaviour. It went really well! Miss Todd congratulated us. She said we were a credit to the school, and she gave us some money for the cats! I was really, really pleased until Petal started off moaning and saying that a good dress rehearsal meant a bad show.

"I beg your pardon, it means nothing of the kind," said Starlotta. "That is just stupid superstition."

One thing about Starlotta, she is a real *trouper*. (One of Auntie Lily's expressions.) You have to admire her.

After school, me and Steffi stayed behind to do a poster. We used one of the computers so that it would look professional and we could make a load of copies. We had decided to call ourselves The Luvvies. It was just a joke, really, to get our own back on Thomas.

The show was *supposed* to be called *Cats' Tales* but Steff went and spelt it *Cats' Tails* by mistake and I thought perhaps that was quite funny, so we left it.

* * * *

Come and see

* * * * * * * *

THE LUVVIES

* **in** *

CATS' TAILS

* **performances at** *

2.30, 3.30 and 4.30

* * * * * * * *

* * * *

Sam's mum didn't seem one little bit grateful when I told her how we were going to make money to rescue the cats.

I said, "Me and my friends at stage school have made this show and we're going to come along to your fair and do it."

Well! You'd have thought she'd at least have said thank you. But she didn't. All she said was, "That's really nice of you, Stevie. You'll have to forgive me, I'm rushed off my feet." And that was it! She put the telephone down.

I'd been going to ask her not to say anything to Sam (in case he told Thomas) only she didn't give me the chance. But somehow I didn't think she would say anything. I didn't think she was that interested. She thought we were just a load of silly little kids, messing around. We would just have to prove her wrong!

When I got home I went up to my room to practise my cat dance one more time. I was a little street cat, playing in the sunshine. I chased my tail, I chased butterflies, I had fun! And then...

Then I ran into the road, and that was when all my troubles began.

The first part of my story was a happy one. I was still in the middle of it when Mum called me to come and have tea, so I danced my way downstairs and into the hall. As I reached the kitchen the door opened and Thomas came out, carrying a glass of orange juice. Well! You can guess what happened. That orange juice went *everywhere*. All down the wall, all over the carpet.

"You idiot!" yelled Thomas.

"Now what's happened?" cried Mum.

"The stupid luvvy's gone and spilt my orange juice!" roared Thomas.

I just put my hands up like cats' paws and went, "Miaow!"

Thomas glowered at me. "What's that s'pposed to be?"

"You'll see!" I said.

Next morning he was in for a *real* surprise.

Oh, but so was I! When I woke up...

Chapter 5

DISASTER! My cheeks were all covered in bright red spots!

"Mum!" I bawled. "*Muuuuum!*"

I went hurtling down the stairs. Mum rushed out of the kitchen.

"Stevie! What on earth is the – oh, my goodness! You've got the chicken pox!"

"I can't have!" I wailed.

"It certainly looks as though you have," said Mum.

Thomas had come down and was skulking in the doorway. "Chicken pox!" he sniggered.

He'd been horrid to me all week. *Really* horrid. It was because he thought I didn't care about the cats.

"It's not funny!" I said.

"I think it is," said Thomas. "You always wanted to be seen in a SPOTlight!"

Oh, ha ha! Very witty, I *don't* think.

"What a nuisance," said Mum. "You'll have to be off school. And I'm sorry, Thomas, but you won't be able to go to the fair this afternoon."

"*Mum!*" We screamed it at her together.

"Not if you've got chicken pox," said Mum.

"*I* haven't got it!" roared Thomas.

"It's only a matter of time. I can't have you going round infecting people. Stevie! Get yourself back to bed. I'd better call the doctor."

"But I'm not *ill*," I said. "I feel perfectly all right!"

"That's funny," said Mum. She put a hand on my forehead. "You don't seem to have a temperature. And those spots..." She peered at them more closely.

"Hm," she said. "That's odd!"

I said, "W-what's odd?"

"Come over here," said Mum.

She marched me across to the sink. Before I could stop her she was scrubbing away at my cheeks as hard as she could go with a scrubbing brush and soap.

"Ow! Ooch! Ouch!" I wriggled like mad but Mum held me in a firm grasp.

"There!" she said. "That's better. Still a bit pink, but I think we can safely say it's not chicken pox."

"So w-w-what is it?" I stammered. I rubbed my hands over my face. It was all zingy and sizzling from where Mum had scrubbed at it. It could be something *fatal*. "What is it?" I screeched.

114

"I'm not quite sure," said Mum. "I wonder if your brother might know?"

"*Thomas?*"

I cornered him in the bathroom. I threatened to spray him all over with Dad's shaving foam if he didn't own up.

"It was a joke!" he said. "It was a joke!"

That *disgusting* boy. He had crept into my room at dead of night and dotted me with beetroot juice. I *hate* beetroot!

"You're such an idiot!" I yelled. "Mum might have made us both stay indoors!"

I'd been going to tell him about *Cats' Tails* but now I decided not to. He was going to be the very LAST PERSON to know about it.

The fair started at two o'clock. Thomas was going to get there early, so he could help people set up their stalls. Me and Steff were going to get there early, too. We wanted to pin up our posters and find ourselves a little corner. We had to get there before Thomas!

"Where are you going?" he said, when he saw me with my coat on.

"Going round to Steff's," I said. "We have things to do. Far more important than your silly old fair!"

I know it was mean of me, but there are times when he just gets me so *mad*.

Steff only lives five minutes away. I was round there in a flash.

"Quick!" I panted, when Steff came to the door. "We've got to get there before Thomas!"

We crammed a bag with our costumes and make-up, snatched the posters and ran. We were lucky! Sam's mum was there, but Thomas hadn't arrived. And Sam was down the far end of the hall and didn't see us. We were still a secret!

Sam's mum was really surprised when she saw our posters. It was like all of a sudden she realised that we weren't just silly little kids. We were professionals!

"My goodness!" she said. "This is most impressive!"

"We did it on the computer," said Steff.

"We want to make loads of money for you," I said. "We've made some already!"

"Well! Where are we going to put you? I know!" Sam's mum clapped her hands. "There's a little stage up there. Would that do?"

A stage! Steffi and me looked at each other. A real stage!

"It's only very tiny, I'm afraid."

"It's only a tiny show," said Steffi.

"But it is *professional*," I assured her.

Sam's mum was right about the stage: it was *really* tiny. More like a little platform.

"But kind of cute," said Steff.

"And it's got a curtain," I said.

We went back into the hall with our posters and

some Blu-Tack and we stuck posters absolutely everywhere. We stuck them on the curtains, we stuck them on the walls, we stuck them on the doors. We even stuck them in the toilets!

On our way back to the stage we bumped into Thomas. He said, "Oh, so you came, after all. You're far too early, we haven't opened yet." And then he caught sight of one of our posters and his jaw dropped. He said, "What's that?"

Me and Steffi studied it.

"Dunno," I said.

"Dunno," said Steff.

Thomas narrowed his eyes. "Are you up to something?"

"What, *us*?" said Steff. And we giggled and linked arms and went strolling off.

We'd told all the others to be there at two o'clock, so as soon as the doors opened we went and stood at the entrance and whispered, "On stage!" each time someone arrived.

Everyone turned up on time, because that is what they teach us at Starlight. "You must never, ever be late for an engagement." If ever any of us is, Miss Todd puts a black mark against our name. Two black marks and you're in trouble. Dead trouble. It means you're not sent for any more auditions for the rest of the term, and if you still don't mend your ways you get THROWN OUT.

It makes me go like jelly just to think of it!

When everybody had arrived, me and Steffi went backstage to get into our costumes and put our make-up on. All the others were already in their costumes. They had travelled in them! But they all carried their tails except for Rosa, who trailed hers behind her, sticking out of her coat. It looked really odd! But Rosa doesn't care. She never cares about things like that.

"If people want to stare, let them," she said.

Thomas stared like mad! His eyes were practically on stalks as Rosa and her tail went swishing down the hall.

Promptly at two-thirty Starlotta stepped out between the curtains and blew on a trumpet she had borrowed from her brother. Starlotta can't actually play the trumpet. All she can do is make braying noises.

"Parp p-p-parp PARP!"

At least it attracted people's attention! Everyone fell silent and turned towards the stage.

"Ladies and gentlemen," announced Starlotta, "we proudly present...The Luvvies, in *Cats' Tails*!"

Then two of us whisked back the curtain and the show began. We came on in turns, to tell our stories. We were old cats, young cats, happy cats, sad cats: cats that were lost, cats that were sick, cats that had been run over.

Dell was an *old* cat; so old that her poor bones creaked every time she moved.

Rosa was a singing cat, trilling her catty songs—until some cruel person chucked a stone at her and broke her leg.

Petal was a lost cat. She miaowed most piteously. Her heartless owners had moved away and left her behind.

Ricky was a tom cat who had been in a fight with a savage dog. Ahmed was attacked by a gang of bullies. Tiffany was starving.

I was a happy cat, playing in the sunshine. But I didn't look where I was going and I ran in front of a car and got knocked down. Nobody bothered to stop and see if I was hurt. They just left me there, in the gutter.

By the end, the stage was full of sad little heaps. Poor little lost kitty cats, crouched in their corners. No one to love us, no one to take care of us.

And then the beautiful rescue lady arrived! She saw us all and she called to us, and one by one we crept up to her. She stroked us and petted us and gave us food and lovely warm beds. And we all started purring and rubbing against her to show how grateful we were.

But, oh, the money ran out! The rescue lady opened her purse and shook it, and it was empty. And we all went "Miaow!" and stretched out our paws, and the rescue lady showed her empty purse to the audience and said, "What am I to do? If someone doesn't help me, all these poor cats will have to go!"

And we all looked as sad as we could and went "Miaaaaaaow!" in our most pathetic voices. And the rescue lady walked forward and held out her purse to the audience.

I have to tell you that it was a BIG purse. A *really* big purse. It was an old handbag belonging to Starlotta's gran and it was the size of a suitcase, practically. But guess what? The audience almost filled it! One lady gave us a twenty pound note. Another lady gave us a cheque. When we looked at it later we found that it was for ONE HUNDRED POUNDS!

Everyone clapped and clapped and we all made little catty bows and rubbed our ears and our whiskers and set up a really loud purring. The best moment of all was when we poured the money into a carrier bag and gave it to Sam's mum. She cried, "Oh, I don't know what to say! This is so marvellous, I can't believe it!"

We couldn't quite believe it, either. We'd hoped to make a lot of money, but we hadn't expected twenty pound notes and a cheque for a hundred!

We did two more performances and after each one the big purse was filled with money.

"Will the cats be safe now?" said Rosa, anxiously.

Sam's mum hugged us all, one after another, and said yes, the cats would be safe. "But maybe next year, if we do another fair, The Luvvies might come back again?"

We promised that we would.

That evening, after tea, Thomas came up to me, all bright red, and muttered, "Sorry I called you a stupid luvvy."

"That's all right," I told him. I mean, I could afford to be generous. I'd helped save the cats.

"I'll tell you what," said Thomas. "When I'm a vet and you're a big star, I'll be sure and tell everyone you're my sister."

"Hey! Wow! Gee whizz!" I said, and I did a pretend faint.

I would never admit it to Thomas, but it was quite the nicest thing he'd ever said to me!

Turn the page for
more books by
Jean Ure that
you might enjoy...

£4.99   1 84121 839 1

The girlfriends are all going to different schools now. The gang meets every Saturday, but suddenly Polly finds she has other invitations, like to her new friend, Chloë's, party.

Who will Polly choose?
Will the girlfriends stick together?

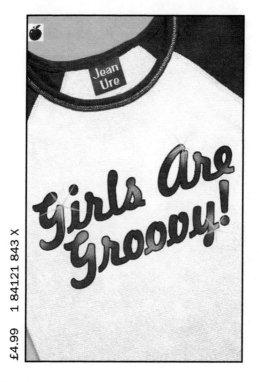

£4.99   1 84121 843 X

Frizz is behaving very strangely.
    Polly is worried that Frizz hates her new
school and feels lonely without the
                    rest of the Gang of Four.

But is Frizz feeling left out,
        or is she the grooviest girl of all?

£4.99   1 84121 847 2

When Polly gets back from summer camp it
seems that all her friends have grown up and
left her behind. Even Frizz is wearing a bra!
And they keep inviting boys to their parties.

Polly hates boys.
But will she decide they're OK in the end?

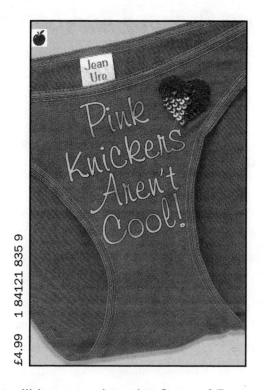

£4.99   1 84121 835 9

What will happen when the Gang of Four
move to new schools?
Will they be able to stick together then?
And will they get rid of Jessamy James,
who wears pink knickers and is just so uncool?

Polly is in for a surprise
at her new school...

More Orchard Red Apples

The Truth Cookie	Fiona Dunbar	1 84362 549 0	£5.99
Cupid Cakes	Fiona Dunbar	1 84362 688 8	£5.99
Chocolate Wishes	Fiona Dunbar	1 84362 689 6	£5.99
Utterly Me, Clarice Bean	Lauren Child	1 84362 304 8	£4.99
Clarice Bean Spells Trouble	Lauren Child	1 84121 920 7	£4.99
The Fire Within	Chris d'Lacey	1 84121 533 3	£5.99
IceFire	Chris d'Lacey	1 84362 373 0	£5.99
My Scary Fairy Godmother	Rose Impey	1 84362 683 7	£4.99
The Shooting Star	Rose Impey	1 84362 560 1	£4.99
Hothouse Flower	Rose Impey	1 84616 215 7	£4.99
Do Not Read This Book	Pat Moon	1 84121 435 3	£4.99
Do Not Read Any Further	Pat Moon	1 84121 456 6	£4.99
Do Not Read Or Else	Pat Moon	1 84616 082 0	£4.99
Tower-block Pony	Alison Prince	1 84121 810 3	£4.99
When Mum Threw Out the Telly	Emily Smith	1 84121 835 9	£4.99
Stevie Silver – Star Light	Jean Ure	1 84121 780 8	£4.99

Orchard Red Apples are available from all good bookshops,
or can be ordered direct from the publisher:
Orchard Books, PO BOX 29, Douglas IM99 1BQ
Credit card orders please telephone 01624 836000
or fax 01624 837033
or visit our Internet site: www.wattspub.co.uk
or e-mail: bookshop@enterprise.net for details.

To order please quote title, author and ISBN
and your full name and address.
Cheques and postal orders should be made payable to 'Bookpost plc.'
Postage and packing is FREE within the UK
(overseas customers should add £1.00 per book).

Prices and availability are subject to change.